Battle
Island

The
Desert
Lands

6.

BEFORE **ANY** GREAT
ADVENTURER EMBARKS
ON THEIR QUEST,
THEY CHECK THEIR MAPS.
YOU SHOULD TOO.

Giants
Quarry

ar. where Onothorn,
on of flames nests.

There are no more
giants

| ARTISTRY | 4 | STRENGTH | 35 |
| CUTENESS | 66 | CUNNING | 47 |

HOODED VULTURE

| COURAGE | 81 | WISDOM | 79 |
| SPEED | 67 | UNIQUE POWERS | 32 |

| ARTISTRY | 15 | STRENGTH | 45 |
| CUTENESS | 5 | CUNNING | 77 |

LORD SINGE

| COURAGE | 6 | WISDOM | 26 |
| SPEED | 17 | UNIQUE POWERS | 71 |

| ARTISTRY | 78 | STRENGTH | 23 |
| CUTENESS | 24 | CUNNING | 71 |

MISS FIREY

| COURAGE | 84 | WISDOM | 57 |
| SPEED | 39 | UNIQUE POWERS | 14 |

| ARTISTRY | 15 | STRENGTH | 11 |
| CUTENESS | 89 | CUNNING | 17 |

SMOKE BAT

| COURAGE | 31 | WISDOM | 43 |
| SPEED | 78 | UNIQUE POWERS | 19 |

| ARTISTRY | 23 | STRENGTH | 36 |
| CUTENESS | 21 | CUNNING | 32 |

GRAHAME

| COURAGE | 59 | WISDOM | 13 |
| SPEED | 45 | UNIQUE POWERS | 16 |

| ARTISTRY | 44 | STRENGTH | 10 |
| CUTENESS | 87 | CUNNING | 12 |

TWO-BUMMED DUCK

| COURAGE | 81 | WISDOM | 17 |
| SPEED | 17 | UNIQUE POWERS | 87 |

| ARTISTRY | 63 | STRENGTH | 38 |
| CUTENESS | 47 | CUNNING | 51 |

MONITOR LIZARD

| COURAGE | 34 | WISDOM | 93 |
| SPEED | 32 | UNIQUE POWERS | 71 |

| ARTISTRY | 99 | STRENGTH | 86 |
| CUTENESS | 39 | CUNNING | 12 |

ONATHORN

| COURAGE | 87 | WISDOM | 50 |
| SPEED | 69 | UNIQUE POWERS | 71 |

| ARTISTRY | 7 | STRENGTH | 17 |
| CUTENESS | 39 | CUNNING | 68 |

ROBBING ROBIN

| COURAGE | 28 | WISDOM | 13 |
| SPEED | 53 | UNIQUE POWERS | 59 |

| ARTISTRY | 99 | STRENGTH | 23 |
| CUTENESS | 48 | CUNNING | 26 |

SWIFT

| COURAGE | 87 | WISDOM | 71 |
| SPEED | 97 | UNIQUE POWERS | 76 |

| ARTISTRY | 11 | STRENGTH | 91 |
| CUTENESS | 69 | CUNNING | 10 |

POLAR BEARATH

| COURAGE | 79 | WISDOM | 16 |
| SPEED | 21 | UNIQUE POWERS | 21 |

| ARTISTRY | 51 | STRENGTH | 10 |
| CUTENESS | 19 | CUNNING | 71 |

CLICKING CROW

| COURAGE | 14 | WISDOM | 79 |
| SPEED | 53 | UNIQUE POWERS | 84 |

ARTISTRY	61	STRENGTH	79
CUTENESS	0	CUNNING	84

GORGELLA

COURAGE	19	WISDOM	23
SPEED	41	UNIQUE POWERS	76

ARTISTRY	99	STRENGTH	86
CUTENESS	76	CUNNING	13

QUIETSCH

COURAGE	79	WISDOM	53
SPEED	63	UNIQUE POWERS	62

ARTISTRY	43	STRENGTH	69
CUTENESS	6	CUNNING	61

G-Smokes
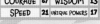

MAGGIE

COURAGE	67	WISDOM	13
SPEED	21	UNIQUE POWERS	17

ARTISTRY	15	STRENGTH	84
CUTENESS	12	CUNNING	68

GORRILATH

COURAGE	39	WISDOM	18
SPEED	56	UNIQUE POWERS	17

ARTISTRY	13	STRENGTH	77
CUTENESS	27	CUNNING	31

CHEF SPARKS

COURAGE	68	WISDOM	31
SPEED	61	UNIQUE POWERS	57

ARTISTRY	16	STRENGTH	81
CUTENESS	16	CUNNING	68

CROCAVILE

COURAGE	31	WISDOM	17
SPEED	19	UNIQUE POWERS	34

ARTISTRY	63	STRENGTH	63
CUTENESS	47	CUNNING	17

INFERNO-LION

COURAGE	92	WISDOM	46
SPEED	71	UNIQUE POWERS	36

ARTISTRY	22	STRENGTH	13
CUTENESS	71	CUNNING	19

NIGHT & GALE

COURAGE	33	WISDOM	47
SPEED	57	UNIQUE POWERS	41

ARTISTRY	56	STRENGTH	57
CUTENESS	59	CUNNING	37

GIANT INK SQUID

COURAGE	36	WISDOM	79
SPEED	41	UNIQUE POWERS	66

ARTISTRY	6	STRENGTH	17
CUTENESS	39	CUNNING	91

DR DINGLEBEE

COURAGE	18	WISDOM	71
SPEED	37	UNIQUE POWERS	68

ARTISTRY	89	STRENGTH	16
CUTENESS	28	CUNNING	50

BLOWPUFF

COURAGE	78	WISDOM	87
SPEED	76	UNIQUE POWERS	67

ARTISTRY	16	STRENGTH	21
CUTENESS	57	CUNNING	31

DRAGON HAWK

COURAGE	72	WISDOM	66
SPEED	92	UNIQUE POWERS	17

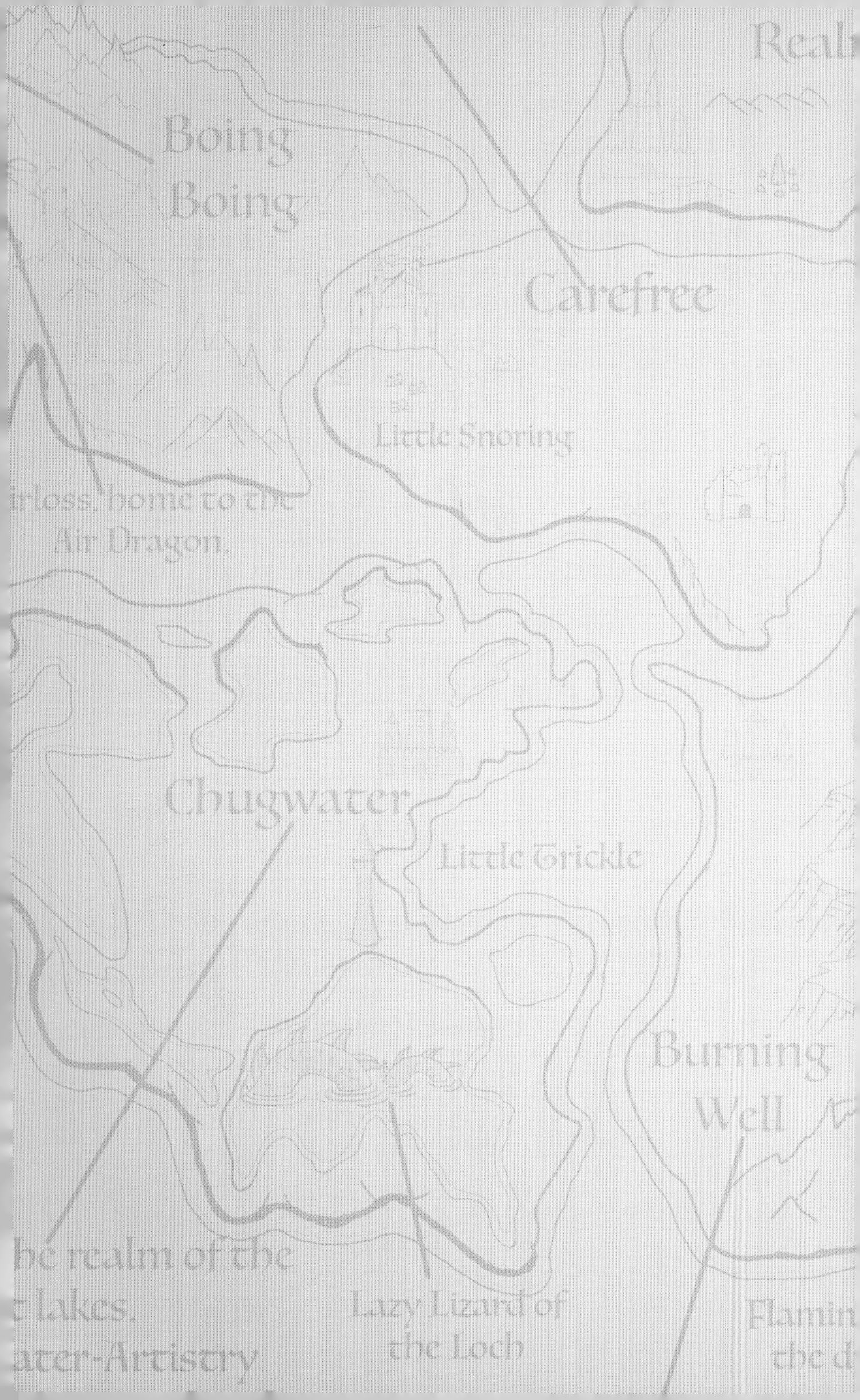

Realm

Boing
Boing

Carefree

Little Snoring

rloss, home to the
Air Dragon,

Chugwater

Little Trickle

Burning
Well

be realm of the
t lakes,
ater-Artistry

Lazy Lizard of
the Loch

Flamin
the

SHERBERT
AND THE
PARTLY DIGESTED
AMULET OF POWER

WRITTEN AND
ILLUSTRATED
BY

F. ARTINGTON

First published in the United Kingdom in 2023 by

Zoomy Books

ISBN 9781915635495

Also available as an eBook

ISBN 9781915635501

Project management by Whitefox

www.wearewhitefox.com

Design by Smart Design Studio

Additional images: iStock.com / Irina Karpinchik.

Printed and bound in Italy by Printer Trento

FSC
www.fsc.org

MIXTE
Papier | Pour une gestion
forestière responsable
FSC® C015829

A Angela, tu eres mi porque

With thanks to those who read the early iterations:

David, Leo, Steffmister G, Lucy, and the
little rainbow dragon Penelope

And a special thanks to

seven-year-old Daniela Harrington
who helped breath life into the illustrations
and inspires and teaches me every day.

NON-FICTION
Noun

Real events, facts and people

FICTION
Noun

Imaginary events, facts and people

THIS STORY IS FICTION. (OR IS IT?)

ZOOMY

WHILE YOU READ THIS BOOK, YOU'LL HAVE THE UNIQUE ABILITY TO MANIPULATE YOUR ARTISTRY.

YOUR ARTISTRY ISN'T THE ABILITY TO MANIPULATE AIR, OR FIRE, LIKE SOME OF THE CHARACTERS IN THIS BOOK. NOR IS TO HOLD SWAY OVER MUD OR SMOKE OR WATER. YOUR ARTISTRY WILL BE THE MOST UNIQUE OF THEM ALL. YOU'LL BE ABLE TO SEE THINGS **NO ONE** IN ALEGNA CAN SEE.

YOU'LL HAVE THE GIFT OF GREAT SIGHT THROUGH ZOOMYS.

FOLLOW THE ARROWS TO JUMP AROUND THE STORY AND FIND OUT SECRETS.

*FOLLOW THE LINE TO FIND OUT WHERE OUR STORY TAKES PLACE.

ZOOMY

ZOOM TO PAGE 10

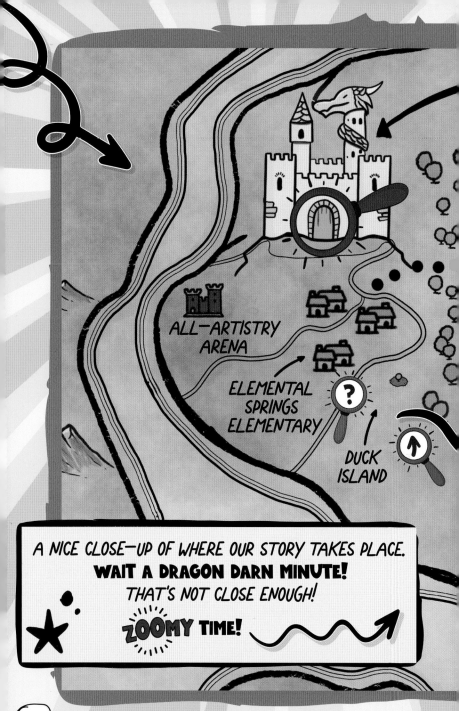

ALL-ARTISTRY ARENA

ELEMENTAL SPRINGS ELEMENTARY

DUCK ISLAND

A NICE CLOSE-UP OF WHERE OUR STORY TAKES PLACE.
WAIT A DRAGON DARN MINUTE!
THAT'S NOT CLOSE ENOUGH!
ZOOMY TIME!

ODD GOINGS ON.
FIND OUT ON PAGE 30

ZOOMY

AGILE EAGLE

NIMBLE NUTCRACKER

LET'S MEET **HATECHI**

LET'S MEET **DIDI**

CHECK OUT THE BOOK'S FLAPS

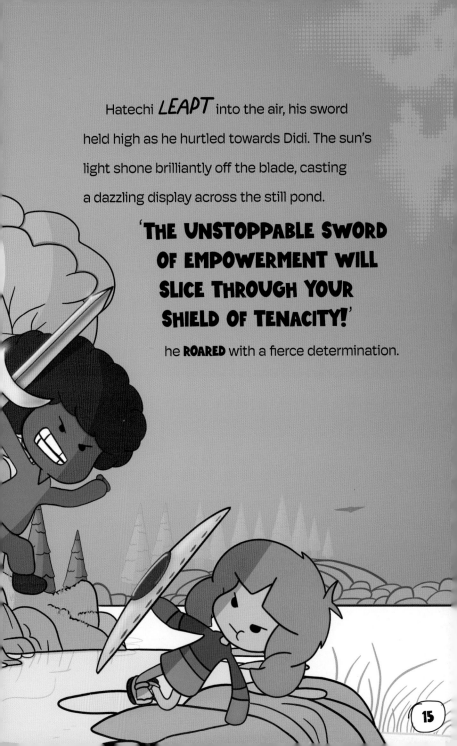

Hatechi *LEAPT* into the air, his sword held high as he hurtled towards Didi. The sun's light shone brilliantly off the blade, casting a dazzling display across the still pond.

'THE UNSTOPPABLE SWORD OF EMPOWERMENT WILL SLICE THROUGH YOUR SHIELD OF TENACITY!'

he **ROARED** with a fierce determination.

Didi was quick to respond.

'**YOU ARE MISTAKEN**,' she cried out, her voice carrying a note of defiance. '*FOR THIS IS NOT THE SHIELD OF TENACITY. IT IS THE SHIELD OF STORMS.*'

As the sword slammed into the shield, Didi let out a mighty '**BOOM!**' that echoed across the landscape. Hatechi was sent flying backwards and skidded to a stop. Undeterred, he tossed the sword into the once calm pond. With a quick motion, he retrieved a dagger from his Cloak of Utilities, its gleaming

edge promising swift and certain victory.

'*THE SHIELD OF STORMS IS NO MATCH FOR THE DAGGER OF TRANQUILLITY!*' Hatechi exclaimed, his eyes glittering with malicious intent as he charged towards Didi once more. Swirling her arms in an attempt to summon the **FORCEFIELD OF TRUTH**, she realised that it was too late. Hatechi had her pinned to the mudbanks, his dagger poised to strike.

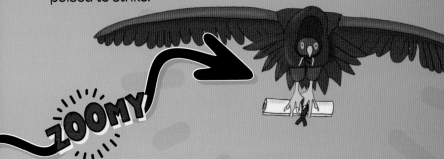

'*HA! THE DAGGER OF TRANQUILLITY WILL BANISH YOU TO A WORLD WITHOUT ARTISTRY. YOU WILL BE FOREVER POWERLESS!*' he cackled, raising the dagger high in the air.

Didi gasped and desperately searched for the **WHIP OF ENDLESS FARTS** or the **SPEAR OF A THOUSAND BURPS**, but neither was within her reach.

'*NOT LIKE THIS!*' she pleaded with Hatechi.

ARTISTRY	4	STRENGTH	35
CUTENESS	66	CUNNING	47

HOODED VULTURE

COURAGE	81	WISDOM	79
SPEED	67	UNIQUE POWERS	32

These intelligent birds are known for their loyalty to the people they choose as their family, and in return for a steady supply of food and a place to call home, they will eagerly lend their wings to that family's needs. With their keen eyesight and remarkable flying ability, the **HOODED VULTURE** serves as a courier, deftly delivering messages and small packages to distant destinations.

At that very moment, a Hooded Vulture screeched from the sky, dropping a scroll onto to the ground next to them.

'*A LETTER FROM HOME*,' Hatechi said.

'**OOOOO!** *A HOODED VULTURE, IT MUST BE IMPORTANT*,' added Didi.

Hatechi dropped the small stick he was holding and reached out his hand, pulling Didi to her feet. '*I ALMOST HAD YOU, SIS*,' he said.

Didi discarded the shield of storms, which was actually just a large crab shell. '*YOU* **CAN'T** *CALL ME SIS*,' she reminded him.

'*IT'S OK HERE. NO ONE WILL COME ANYWHERE NEAR OUR SECRET HIDEOUT, THANKS TO THE DUCKS,*' Hatechi said.

Hatechi's confidence immediately waned as the still water began to stir. At first, it was just a ripple, but soon a full-blown **WHIRLPOOL** appeared.

'*WHAT'S GOING ON?*' asked Didi nervously.

'*CAN A POND BREAK?*' Hatechi asked.

An **ENORMOUS** serpent-like creature came crashing out of the water, its eyes wide and its face purple. It fell onto the mud banks, wheezing heavily and struggling for breath.

'**WHAT ON ALEGNA IS THAT?**' Didi yelped.

'*UNLESS THERE'S A CREATURE CALLED A SLUG—HIPPO—SERPENT, THEN I HAVE NO IDEA!*'

'BUT WHATEVER IT IS, I THINK IT'S CHOKING.'

'IF IT'S CHOKING, WE NEED TO SMASH IT ON ITS CHEST!'
said Didi as she approached the creature.

'BUT WHERE'S ITS CHEST?' asked Hatechi.

'HOW SHOULD I KNOW? JUST GRAB IT AND SQUEEZE!'
said Didi.

They put their arms around where they *THOUGHT*
the animal's chest was and squeezed with all their
might. But to their horror, the creature continued
to wheeze and splutter.

'**WHAT NOW?**' Didi asked.

Hatechi ran to the serpent's large hippo-like
mouth and heaved it open.

'QUICK, CAN YOU SEE ANYTHING LODGED IN IT?' panted
Hatechi.

'**YES!**' Didi exclaimed. She reached into the warm,
moist, earthy smelling mouth and yanked out a
large stick.

Hatechi and Didi weren't quite sure what happened next but their best guess was that this strange creature had *THROWN UP* on top of them!

As they lay there covered in a revolting muddy SLIME, they were relieved to see that the serpent-thingy was no longer wheezing. Unfortunately, that relief was short-lived as the creature reared up and let out an **ANGRY-SOUNDING BURP**. Didi was still clasping the large stick.

'*IS THIS STICK THE PRETEND SWORD OF EMPOWERMENT?*' she asked.

'**WHOOPS!**' Hatechi exclaimed. The animal snarled.

'*IF WE GET EATEN, THIS GOOD DEED WILL GO DOWN AS THE WORST IN HISTORY!*' Hatechi said.

Luckily, the creature's grimace quickly turned to a smile. An extremely big smile due to its extensive jaw. Out flopped a slimy tongue, and within a split second, that tongue was smothering Hatechi and Didi's faces.

'*THAT TICKLES,*' laughed Hatechi.

'*I THINK WE'VE MADE A NEW FRIEND,*' Didi giggled.

The sun sparkled off the creature's slimy

scales as it nodded in agreement.

'*WHAT SHALL WE CALL HIM?*' Hatechi asked.

'**HOW ABOUT SHERBERT?** *AS IN SLIMY AND BRIGHT?*'
Didi suggested.

'*PERFECT!*' Hatechi exclaimed.

Sherbert let out a **BURP**.

'*HE SEEMS TO LIKE IT TOO,*'
Hatechi said.

The next hour flew
by as the three
played *WARRIORS* and
*GOBLINS, WIZARDS AND
WITCHES*, and *THE CIRCLE
OF DRAGONS*, which was
by far their new friend's
favourite. Hatechi and
Didi had so much fun
that it wasn't until

the golden light of the upcoming sunset shone across the pond that they realised the time.

'WE'VE GOT TO HEAD BACK TO OUR DORMS NOW, SHERBERT,' Didi said. 'BUT FEEL FREE TO SLEEP IN OUR SECRET TREE HOUSE.'

And Sherbert smiled as he slithered around his new friends and then shot up the tree to the tree house.

'BEST DAY **EVER!**' Didi said as they made their way back to school.

'*BIG TIME,*' agreed Hatechi as he unrolled the message scroll from home and began to read it.

'*WHAT'S IT SAY?*' Didi asked.

Hatechi looked up at his sister, a tear forming in his eye. '*TURNS OUT IT'S NOT THE BEST DAY EVER, DIDI,*' he said, passing her the letter.

z z z Z Z

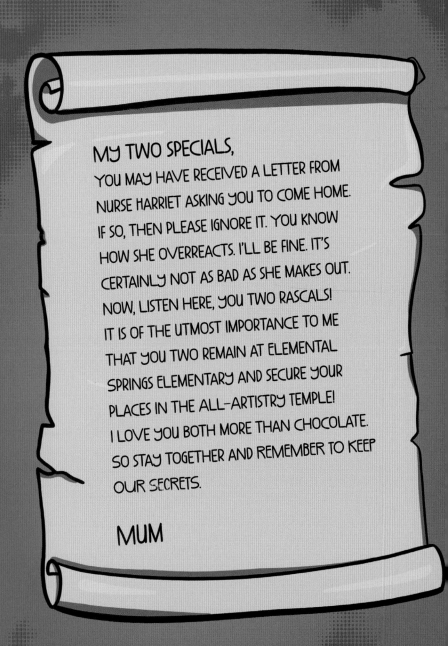

MY TWO SPECIALS,
YOU MAY HAVE RECEIVED A LETTER FROM
NURSE HARRIET ASKING YOU TO COME HOME.
IF SO, THEN PLEASE IGNORE IT. YOU KNOW
HOW SHE OVERREACTS. I'LL BE FINE. IT'S
CERTAINLY NOT AS BAD AS SHE MAKES OUT.
NOW, LISTEN HERE, YOU TWO RASCALS!
IT IS OF THE UTMOST IMPORTANCE TO ME
THAT YOU TWO REMAIN AT ELEMENTAL
SPRINGS ELEMENTARY AND SECURE YOUR
PLACES IN THE ALL-ARTISTRY TEMPLE!
I LOVE YOU BOTH MORE THAN CHOCOLATE.
SO STAY TOGETHER AND REMEMBER TO KEEP
OUR SECRETS.

MUM

TWO YEARS LATER

Chapter 1

Last Year, Last Chance

Two years had passed since Didi and Hatechi had become friends with Sherbert. Despite Sherbert's subtle guidance, Didi and Hatechi remained at the bottom of their class.

As their final year at Elemental Springs Elementary approached, their mum's last wish, that they receive the *HONOUR OF ADMITTANCE* to the esteemed secondary school, the **ALL-ARTISTRY TEMPLE**, looked bleak indeed. But all was not lost (yet).

Didi and Hatechi had a plan.

'*THERE IT IS, HATECHI,*' said Didi, gazing up at the distant towering spires of the All-Artistry Temple, the sun dipping below the tallest of the towers.

'*MAGICAL!*' agreed Hatechi, transfixed.

Nestled among the mountains, the **ALL-ARTISTRY TEMPLE** was home to five departments. From their vantage point, Hatechi and Didi could only see two – the Water Department, perched on the edge of a glittering lake with waterfalls cascading from its thick brick walls, and the Air Department, with its magnificent white granite façade soaring high above the rest.

'*TOMORROW'S OUR* **LAST CHANCE** *TO SECURE OUR PLACES THERE,*' said Hatechi.

'**YES.** *IF ALL GOES TO PLAN AT THE ELEMENTAL GAME,*' said Didi hopefully.

The **ELEMENTAL GAMES** were a momentous occasion that marked the beginning of the new school year.

For students like Hatechi and Didi, who had struggled to shine during term time, the Games were a **LAST CHANCE** to prove themselves worthy of a coveted spot at the **ALL-ARTISTRY TEMPLE**.

'*YEAH, ABOUT THAT,*' said Hatechi nervously. '*THERE ARE KIDS THAT GO TO THE ALL—ARTISTRY TEMPLE THAT CAN MANIPULATE THEIR ARTISTRY SO WELL THEY CAN JUMP AS HIGH AS BUILDINGS, CHANGE CURRENTS IN RIVERS,*

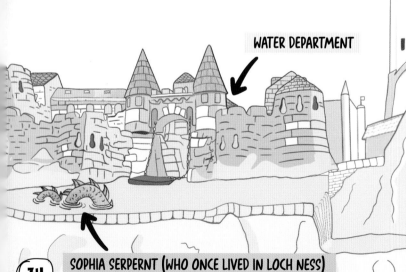

WATER DEPARTMENT

SOPHIA SERPERNT (WHO ONCE LIVED IN LOCH NESS)

FILL ROOMS FULL OF SMOKE, ADJUST THE SOIL THEY WALK ON, AND TURN CANDLES INTO FLAME THROWERS.'

'**WHAT'S YOUR POINT?**' demanded Didi, her hands planted firmly on her hips.

'ALL I CAN DO WITH MY AIR ARTISTRY IS MAKE PEOPLE **FART**!' said Hatechi, his thick brown curls wobbling as he gestured to Didi. 'AND WITH YOUR WATER ARTISTRY, YOU SHOULD AT LEAST BE ABLE TO CREATE A CURRENT IN A PUDDLE BY NOW.'

'**HEY!** I CAN MAKE PEOPLE **WET THEMSELVES, THOUGH!**' Didi exclaimed.

AIR DEPARTMENT

AN AIR-ARTISTRY PUPIL DOING THEIR THING

'WHICH HAS COME IN HANDY NEVER.' Hatechi huffed.

'DON'T YOU THINK IT MAY RAISE SUSPICION IF WE WIN ALL

THE EVENTS AT THE ELEMENTARY GAMES?'

'THE WHOLE POINT IS TO BE NOTICED,' explained Didi.

'ANYWAY, I'VE READ THE RULE BOOK, AND WE'LL HAVE TO

SETTLE FOR WINNING FOUR OF THE FIVE EVENTS.'

Hatechi raised an eyebrow.

Didi stared knowingly at Hatechi. *'YOU DID READ THE RULE BOOK, DIDN'T YOU?'* she asked.

Hatechi fidgeted nervously. *'I TRIED, BUT I KEPT FALLING ASLEEP. SO MANY OLD WORDS!'* Hatechi said.

*'IF YOU HAD READ THE RULE BOOK, YOU WOULDN'T BE SO WORRIED. IT STATES WE CAN USE **ARTISTRY POWER** IN ANY WAY, IN ANY FORM, FROM ANY SOURCE! I THINK ANY SOURCE MEANS MUD, AIR, WATER AND SO ON. HOWEVER, IT DOESN'T SPECIFY AT ANY POINT THAT THE ARTISTRY SOURCE CAN'T BE A MAGICAL SERPENT*

SLUG! IT ONLY SPECIFIES THAT THE USE OF ARTISTRY MUST NEVER ENDANGER ANOTHER CONTESTANT. WHICH IS WHY WE'LL ONLY WIN FOUR OUT OF THE FIVE EVENTS, AS I CAN'T THINK OF A WAY TO WIN AT **AIR SLING** SAFELY.'

'THAT SHOULD BE MORE THAN ENOUGH,' Hatechi said, his concerned grimace turning into a smile. 'PROFESSOR BLOWPUFF WOULD HAVE TO ACCEPT US INTO THE **ALL-ARTISTRY TEMPLE!** AND IF YOU SAY WE'RE NOT CHEATING, THEN WE'RE NOT CHEATING.'

'**WE'RE NOT!**' Didi exclaimed, then looked up towards the shimmering temple and inhaled deeply. 'BUT TO PULL THIS OFF, WE CAN'T RISK GETTING CAUGHT. IF WE DON'T GET INTO THE **ALL-ARTISTRY TEMPLE,** WE'LL BE HOMELESS. WE CAN'T RETURN TO THE DESERT LANDS, THERE'S NO ONE THERE FOR US NOW. BESIDES, LOOK AT US! WE'RE CLEARLY NOT FROM THERE. I HAVE WEBBED FEET, FOR DRAGONS' SAKE!'

Hatechi flashed a wry smile and looked at Didi lovingly. He pointed to himself.

'I think it's pretty obvious where we each should hail from.' Hatechi then looked around before lowering his voice. *'SOMETIMES I THINK MUM USED TO WORRY TOO MUCH ABOUT OUR SECRET. NO ONE WOULD BELIEVE WE'RE TWINS ANYWAY.'*

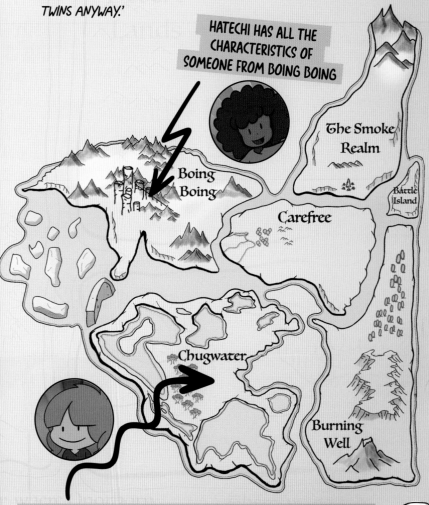

HATECHI HAS ALL THE CHARACTERISTICS OF SOMEONE FROM BOING BOING

The Smoke Realm

Battle Island

Boing Boing

Carefree

Chugwater

Burning Well

DIDI HAS ALL THE CHARACTERISTICS OF SOMEONE FROM CHUGWATER

Didi offered a resigned shrug, her expression tinged with a hint of sorrow. '*MUM HAD HER REASONS, I SUPPOSE. ALL THAT MATTERED TO HER BY THE END WAS GUARDING OUR SECRET AND ENSURING OUR ACCEPTANCE INTO THE* **ALL-ARTISTRY TEMPLE**. *TOMORROW WE'LL FULFIL HER DREAM.*'

At that moment, a loud **BURP** erupted from the trees behind them, startling Hatechi and Didi.

Emerging from the shadows, a strange creature slithered across the gravel path, its body glistening with slime. Rearing up like a cobra, it bared its massive hippopotamus-like jaw, spewing a torrent of slippery goo, then it glided towards Hatechi and Didi at lightning speed, its enormous flat tail churning the ground beneath it.

'**SHERBERT!**' Hatechi and Didi exclaimed in delight and relief, their faces lighting up as they hugged their friend.

'*YOU NEED TO STAY HIDDEN, BOY,*' said Didi. Then with a nod in the direction of the **TEMPLE** in the distance, she said, '*THAT'S WHAT IT'S ALL ABOUT, SHERBERT. TOMORROW,*

YOU'LL PLAY A BIG ROLE IN HELPING US SECURE OUR PLACES. AFTER THAT, ALL WE'LL NEED TO DO IS STAY OUT OF TROUBLE FOR THE LAST YEAR AT ELEMENTAL SPRINGS,' said Didi.

'**STAY OUT OF TROUBLE FOR A YEAR?** WINNING THE ELEMENTAL GAMES WILL BE THE EASY BIT,' said Hatechi.

Didi and Hatechi burst out laughing, and Sherbert

joined in with a series of happy gargles.

Didi went through the plan with Hatechi and Sherbert. **FINALLY**, the trio were ready to take on the Elemental Games.

| ARTISTRY | 80 | STRENGTH | 30 |
| CUTENESS | 85 | CUNNING | 41 |

SHERBERT

| COURAGE | 86 | WISDOM | 67 |
| SPEED | 82 | UNIQUE POWERS | 71 |

SHERBERT is incredibly fast underwater and in mud, thanks to his large, strong, flat tail. He's also capable of producing and expelling a slippery transparent slime when he chooses to. With his big eyes he can see through the murkiest water or even a dark room full of smoke. sherbert takes great pride in his ability to spit mud, which he uses to create beautiful sculptures.

Chapter 2

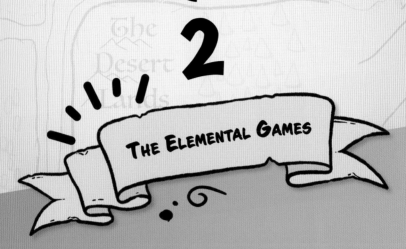

THE ELEMENTAL GAMES

A soft, tepid easterly breeze flowed through the open-air stadium where the Elemental Games were about to start. A **BUZZ** of excitement filled the stands as the pupils from the prestigious **ALL-ARTISTRY TEMPLE** arrived and filed towards their seats. Hatechi and Didi were huddled behind a bollard, peering out and watching the stadium fill up.

'BLIMEY, IT'S LOOKING BUSY OUT THERE. YOU SURE WE CAN DO THIS?' asked Hatechi.

'**ABSOLUTELY!** *THIS WILL BE MORE FUN THAN WHEN WE FILLED A BOUNCY CASTLE WITH BUBBLE MIXTURE,*' laughed Didi nervously as she flicked her orange fringe restlessly from her eyes.

'*YEAH!*' sniggered Hatechi, feverishly tapping his foot. '*AND IT WILL BE BETTER THAN THAT TIME WE PUT A FAKE MOUSTACHE ON MISS FIREY'S DRINKING CUP.*'

At that moment, a shadow crept over them, and as it did so, Hatechi and Didi began to sweat. In Alegna, some shadows bring smoke and some wind. This shadow brought fire.

'*MORNING, MISS FIREY,*' said Hatechi and Didi in unison.

Miss Firey was the tallest headteacher that Elemental Springs Elementary had ever had (*PROBABLY*). Her golden eyes, which she was incredibly proud of, appeared like raging fire as she looked down at her two least favourite pupils.

| ARTISTRY | 78 | STRENGTH | 23 |
| CUTENESS | 24 | CUNNING | 71 |

MISS FIREY

| COURAGE | 84 | WISDOM | 57 |
| SPEED | 39 | UNIQUE POWERS | 14 |

At Elemental Springs Elementary, **MISS FIREY** reigns as the formidable headteacher. She hails from the scorching plains of Burning Well and has the power to command fire. She is not shy about displaying her prowess and can often be seen twirling fireballs in her palms, casting an awe-inspiring spectacle for all who behold.

Everything about Miss Firey was raging, from her blazing red hair to her dragon-blood mascara. Wearing her usual dark grey fireproof gown, she snorted through her long curved nose and said with a nasal snigger, '**GETTING NERVOUS, ARE YOU?** I'M SURE YOU WON'T COME LAST IN ALL THE EVENTS.'

Then she let out a heated breath.

'ONE MORE YEAR, AND I'LL NEVER HAVE TO SEE YOUR TWO ORDINARY FACES IN MY SCHOOL AGAIN. NOW, **CHOP, CHOP.** THE AIR SLING EVENT IS ABOUT TO START.'

Chapter 3

AIR SLING

Hatechi and Didi came in last and second to last in the Air Sling event.

'*WELL, IT COULD HAVE BEEN WORSE,*' sniggered Miss Firey. '**OH, WAIT!** *NO, IT COULDN'T HAVE!*'

Didi ground her teeth. Hatechi made fists.

'*IT'S SHOW TIME,*' whispered Didi.

'*BIG TIME!*' agreed Hatechi.

Once the next event, Floor Is Larva, was over, Miss Firey had a face like she was chewing a Bumble Wee. She was so puzzled that Hatechi and Didi had won gold and silver that she didn't notice the peculiar mud on Hatechi and Didi's feet. After the thrilling event Plunge, Miss Firey was stunned to once again present

ARTISTRY	15	STRENGTH	11
CUTENESS	89	CUNNING	17

SMOKE BAT

COURAGE	31	WISDOM	43
SPEED	78	UNIQUE POWERS	19

With its ability to shroud itself in a veil of smoke, the **SMOKE BAT** is a master of concealment. Its eyes, large and luminous, are perfectly adapted to the darkness, allowing it to see with crystal clarity where others would struggle.

Hatechi and Didi with gold and silver medals. Her suspicion was surely heightened after witnessing the incredible spectacle **THE CHAMBER OF SMOKE**. Not only did Hatechi and Didi manage to secure the top spots once more, but they also broke the all-time speed record set by a **SMOKE BAT**. Such a remarkable feat left everyone amazed and confused.

As the final event loomed, Hatechi and Didi were steadfast in their conviction that winning was the key to securing their places at the **ALL-ARTISTRY TEMPLE**. The challenge, aptly named Mud Shield, promised to push both competitors to their limits. Little did they know that Miss Firey had her own plans in mind.

Chapter 4

Mud Shield

Mud Shield had only ever been won by a creature called a Gumbo. A Gumbo is a unique species that resembles humans but is taller, has less body fat, and SLIGHTLY larger ears. Gumbos can only utilise one Artistry. **MUD ARTISTRY** is a rare talent and few creatures other than Gumbos can use it. Obviously, the headteacher of the **ALL-ARTISTRY TEMPLE**, Professor Blowpuff, has mastered it, but he has mastered EVERYTHING!

| ARTISTRY | 23 | STRENGTH | 36 |
| CUTENESS | 21 | CUNNING | 32 |

GRAHAME

| COURAGE | 59 | WISDOM | 13 |
| SPEED | 45 | UNIQUE POWERS | 16 |

GRAHAME GILBERTHAIR is a Gumbo and because he can manipulate his Artistry outwards, he holds sway over mud. With a flourish of his arms, he can unleash a flurry of mud balls.

So there was no way Hatechi or Didi could excel at **MUD ARTISTRY**. Therefore, Miss Firey believed that she was about to catch them out. Her nostrils flared and she tilted her head back and rubbed her hands together in anticipation of their failure.

'*I'M ABOUT TO* **MUDdle** *WITH YOU TWO!*' she muttered, allowing herself a little cackle.

Several Gumbos had prepared the arena by creating a rectangle of knee-deep shimmery mud. All the students stood on the sidelines waiting for Miss Firey to call out the contestants. '**HATECHI!**' she shouted.

Hatechi waded to the middle of the muddy pitch. He and Didi knew that Miss Firey would pick one of them first. They also knew that if she had any sense, she would face them off against each other.

Which meant she wouldn't. Miss Firey would, without a doubt, pick Grahame Gillberthair.

He was a seven-and-a-half-foot-tall Gumbo, had more muscles than most adults, and was so good at Mud Shield that he had already played in the pro league. Miss Firey appeared to be holding back a snigger as she called out his name.

As the gargantuan Grahame strode out to the middle, Hatechi gulped nervously. But when he spotted several muddy bubbles popping just in front of him, a knowing smile crossed his face.

'*GOOD BOY, SHERBERT,*'

he whispered.

Miss Firey signalled the start of the match with a **BLAST** of flames. Grahame had already sent a mud ball hurtling at Hatechi, who winced as it spun towards him at great speed, specks of liquid dirt flying. The audience was engrossed, as if thousands of breaths were held waiting for the inevitable. Didi found

herself *SMILING*, because she knew something the audience didn't.

It was then that Didi spotted someone, or *SOMETHING*, in the audience that sent a shiver down her spine: a figure with wisps of smoke in its hood who was ignoring the spectacle and staring right at her. Didi shuddered.

ZOOMYED FROM PAGE 30

WE NEED A CLOSER LOOK

ZOOMY TO PAGE 61

COULD THIS BE THE CHAP IN THE CROWD?

GASPS filled the stadium. Didi looked back to Hatechi. Just as it seemed like the glorious mud ball swirling through the air was about to slap straight into his face, a shield of mud shot up in front of him, absorbing the ball with ease. Hatechi smiled.

'I KNEW YOU WOULDN'T LET ME DOWN, SHERBERT,' he said.

And he was just about to give Sherbert the signal to launch a mud ball at Grahame when he heard a **CLAP, CLAP, CLAP** come from the otherwise silent crowd. Hatechi looked over to the source of the claps and saw a hooded figure. With each **CLAP**, the smoke swirling around its hood momentarily cleared to reveal the most hideous grin.

WHAT'S THAT ARM ON THE LEFT? ZOOM OUT A LITTLE.

ZOOMY

ZOOM TO PAGE 93

SMASH! A giant mud ball hit the now dry shield in front of Hatechi, causing it to shatter.

'*QUICK, SHERBERT,* **NOW**,' said Hatechi as he reached down.

Then, *SWOOSH!* A muddy ball was flying at a speed that was hard to comprehend and before Hatechi had time to blink, Grahame Gilberthair was knocked flying. Hatechi had won!

He had beaten the favourite. Everything after that was a formality. First, Hatechi and Didi knocked out all the other contestants. Then, when they faced off in the final, they decided to share the winner's medal, which had never been done before.

Proceedings ended, and the whole of the **ALL-ARTISTRY TEMPLE** and Elemental Springs Elementary crowd left in a murmuring mumble of disappointment.

Chapter 5

There is an old fable, a superstitious story well known in Alegna called **Dirty Ducks**, that claims ducks carry diseases (*THEY DON'T*). Because of this factually incorrect chronicle, most Alegnans avoid ducks.

Didi and Hatechi, however, loved ducks. Ducks could fly, swim and walk. Well, more of a waddle than a walk but it worked. It was almost as if ducks had Air *and* Water Artistry, just like Didi and Hatechi. And it doesn't get much more stupendous than when ducks land on the water by skimming across its surface.

HAIRY OVAL HEAD

LESSER-SPOTTED WIND POPPER

MOODY TWO-FOOTED COMPLAINER

BEWARE OF THE DUCKS

MAJOR PARTY POOPER

TWO-BUMMED DUCK

There was also another reason why Didi and Hatechi appreciated ducks. Thanks to the tale **Dirty Ducks**, their secret tree house, which was on a duck island, would *REMAIN* a secret.

In this hideout, they would often make tremendous and outrageous plans to become the greatest Masters of Artistry that ever lived.

There were at least twenty different duck species on this small island. DUCKS WITH LONG NECKS. **Ducks with pompoms on their heads**. RAINBOW DUCKS. **Two-Headed Ducks**, and the rare **TWO-BUMMED DUCK**. The Two-Bummed Duck had no predators because it could fart methane from one bum and a spark from the other bum, thus creating dragon-like fire! The Two-Bummed Duck was a grumpy old so-and-so. Didi believed the grumpiness was caused by its embarrassing name and that the Two-Bummed Duck would be far happier if it was known to the world of Alegna as the **DRAGON DUCK** or the **FIRE DUCK**. Hatechi

| ARTISTRY | 46 | STRENGTH | 10 |
| CUTENESS | 87 | CUNNING | 12 |

TWO-BUMMED DUCK

| COURAGE | 81 | WISDOM | 17 |
| SPEED | 17 | UNIQUE POWERS | 87 |

Whilst the **TWO-BUMMED DUCK** may be cantankerous and quick to anger, it holds a certain renown among its feathered peers. Indeed, there are few things as reassuring to a duck colony as the presence of a member capable of farting fire.

thought differently. He believed the Two-Bummed Duck was bad-tempered because it could never have a sneaky fart without the whole island knowing about it!

Submerged just under the pond water were several hidden stepping stones. Hatechi leapt from the last one onto the muddy bank, quickly followed by Didi.

WASPUG

'WE WON FOUR EVENTS,' said Hatechi.

'I TOLD YOU WE COULD PULL IT OFF.' Didi began to giggle as she leapt off the last stepping stone and onto the island. 'THEY DIDN'T HAVE A CLUE HOW WE DID IT! DID YOU SEE MISS FIREY'S FACE? IT WAS LIKE A WASPUG IN AUTUMN.'

Hatechi let out a howl of laughter.

'AT ONE POINT, SHE LOOKED LIKE A LIBRARIAN AT A HEAVY METAL CONCERT!'

'NOW THEY'LL **HAVE** TO ACCEPT US INTO THE ALL—ARTISTRY TEMPLE NEXT YEAR,' Didi said triumphantly. 'AND I THINK IT'S TIME TO CONGRATULATE TODAY'S TRUE WINNER.'

'**BIG TIME!**' grinned Hatechi.

They approached the water's edge and glanced around. Then, bending down, they reached out with their hands and softly placed them on the top of the water.

'**SHERBERT!**' they called.

Chapter 6

BEING WATCHED

The surface of the pond stirred and the water rippled. Sherbert's head broke the surface. He made a gargling noise and burped, then slid up the mudbank.

'*HELLO, SHERBERT,*' said Hatechi.

'*FANTASTIC WORK, BOY,*' said Didi.

The creature spat a mud ball and flapped his broad tail up and down. Hatechi and Didi put their medals around Sherbert's neck and Sherbert made a **RUMBLING** purr sound.

The sun was lowering and had reached the treeline opposite, creating both a cosy redness that smudged the sky, and a sharp glint across the water. Hatechi and Didi hugged their friend and enjoyed his warmth. The glistening sparkle on top of the pond began to look like tiny bouncing stars. It was only then that Hatechi and Didi thought they spotted movement in the reeds and the mudbank on the other side of the pond.

Chapter 7

The Other Side Of The Pond

Hidden in the reeds was Miss Firey, who was looking even more disgusted than usual.

'**WOW!** *THAT SLIMY—SLUG THING IS REVOLTING! SURELY IT ISN'T WHAT I THINK IT IS, IS IT?*' she muttered to herself.

And hidden in the mudbank lay Grahame Gillberthair, who was looking extremely excited.

'**WOW!** *THAT IS BEAUTIFUL! SURELY THAT ISN'T WHAT I THINK IT IS, IS IT?*' he said to himself.

WORST CAMOUFLAGE EVER!

Chapter
8

IT ACTUALLY COULD
POSSIBLY BE WHAT THEY
THOUGHT IT WAS

The following morning, Hatechi and Didi met in
the passage that linked their respective chambers
to the **GRAND COURTYARD**, which led to their **HUTS OF
LEARNING**. It was a daily ritual. Sleep was the only time
they were apart. And ever since they'd been sleeping
in separate dorms they'd not once woken up
energised. They now walked side by side with a clear
objective as well as a feeling of slight apprehension
following their triumph at the Games.

'*MORNING, CHAMP, HOW'D YOU SLEEP?*' asked Didi through a yawn.

'*I WAS SO TIRED I DIDN'T EVEN GET INTO BED. I WOKE UP THIS MORNING IN THE DORMITORY HALL'S FIREPLACE,*' Hatechi said as he pulled a stick from his hair.

'*I GUESS WE BOTH SLEPT LIKE LOGS THEN! EXHAUSTING BEING CHAMPIONS ISN'T IT?*' said Didi.

As the two winners entered the main entrance of **ELEMENTAL SPRINGS ELEMENTARY**, they immediately heard one of the Monitor Lizards summoning them to the headteacher's office.

ARTISTRY	63	STRENGTH	38
CUTENESS	47	CUNNING	51

MONITOR LIZARD

COURAGE	36	WISDOM	93
SPEED	32	UNIQUE POWERS	71

In the Northern Woodlands of Many Names, the **MONITOR LIZARDS** keep to their ancient tradition and do not leave the woods until they reach their hundredth birthday. During this time, they are taught the sacred art of Observation and Documentation of the events that happen within the realm of the Woodlands.

Miss Firey's office had flagstone floors, stone walls and a stone ceiling. A bulging glass-doored bookcase covered one of the walls. The glass was presumably to protect the books from going up in **FLAMES** when Miss Firey lost her temper, which was not uncommon! She even had a stone desk, behind which she now sat on her stone chair, sunlight shining on her hair from the window behind.

It was then that Didi and Hatechi noticed that Miss Firey had the oddest thing on her face. This might not be Miss Firey after all, because the woman behind that stone desk was smiling! They had never seen Miss Firey smile. **NEVER**. However, the *smile* quickly turned into an evil grin. Hatechi and Didi exhaled. Now they were sure it was her.

'WHY DO YOU TWO LOOK SO RELIEVED?' demanded Miss Firey.

'SORRY, MISS. IT WAS THAT SMILE. IT LOOKED LIKE TEETH ON A PARROT,' said Didi.

'YEAH,' said Hatechi, 'LIKE BALLET SHOES ON A BULL. IT JUST WASN'T RIGHT.'

Miss Firey's neck elongated like an angry snake.

'OH, IT DID, DID IT!? WELL, GET USED TO IT. ALL THESE YEARS I WOULD HAVE LOVED TO CATCH YOU TWO UP TO YOUR CHILDISH TRICKS. IF ONLY I'D THOUGHT OF FOLLOWING YOU SOONER.'

Didi and Hatechi glanced at each other nervously. Miss Firey continued.

'YEAR ONE, WHEN THE ELEMENTAL SPRINGS ELEMENTARY'S DOGS STARTED TO MEOW AND THE CATS STARTED BARKING. YEAR TWO, WHEN ONE MORNING THE MAIN HALL WAS UNEXPECTEDLY TURNED INTO AN ICE RINK. AND YEAR THREE, WHEN THE PURIFYING POOLS TURNED PINK AND ALL THE TEACHERS MYSTERIOUSLY LOST THEIR VOICES! AND, OF COURSE, THE DAY I HAD MY INTERVIEW AT THE ALL-ARTISTRY TEMPLE!'

| ARTISTRY | 13 | STRENGTH | 77 |
| CUTENESS | 27 | CUNNING | 31 |

CHEF SPARKS

| COURAGE | 68 | WISDOM | 31 |
| SPEED | 61 | UNIQUE POWERS | 57 |

Like all scorched stink Lizards, **CHEF SPARKS** comes from the scorched Lands and has the ability to release an odour that smells like boiling broccoli custard. Armed with thick scaly skin he's comfortable in the hottest of kitchens.

'*THAT WASN'T US, MISS,*' Hatechi said. '*THAT WAS CHEF SPARKS! HALF THE SCHOOL HAD THE FARTS!*'

'**QUIET!**' Miss Firey barked. '*FINALLY, I HAVE PROOF OF ONE OF YOUR MISDEMEANOURS!*'

Didi and Hatechi gulped, their eyes widened and they started to fidget nervously. Miss Firey smirked, her eyes piercing, and she leaned forward like a cat edging towards its prey.

'*WHAT IF I WERE TO TELL THE WHOLE OF THE ALL—ARTISTRY TEMPLE HOW YOU TWO BELOW—AVERAGE GOOD—FOR—NOTHINGS MANAGED TO DO SO WELL AT THE ELEMENTAL GAMES?*'

Didi gasped. '*WE DIDN'T BREAK ANY RULES!*'

'**ARE YOU ONE HUNDRED PER CENT SURE ABOUT THAT?**' Miss Firey sneered.

Hatechi looked towards Didi with hope in his eyes.

'*UMM, YES?*' Didi replied.

'*NOT SO SURE NOW, ARE YOU, MISSY?*' laughed Miss Firey.

'*WE COULD BE EXPELLED,*' Hatechi gasped.

'**EXPULSION WOULD BE THE LEAST OF YOUR WORRIES!**'
blasted Miss Firey. '*YOU DO REALISE THAT THIS ELEMENTAL
GAMES WAS THE LAST OPPORTUNITY FOR GRAHAME GILLBERTHAIR
TO BREAK THE ALL-TIME MEDAL TALLY? DO YOU KNOW WHY HIS
NICKNAME IS GRAHAME THE EXECUTIONER?*'

'*I'VE NEVER HEARD ANYONE CALL HIM THAT,*' said Didi.

Miss Firey grinned.

'*NO ONE DARES SAY IT OUT LOUD ANY MORE BECAUSE THE LAST
PERSON TO CALL HIM THAT MYSTERIOUSLY VANISHED.*'

Hatechi and Didi gulped.

Miss Firey moved closer and lowered her voice.

'*DO YOU REMEMBER THE SNOTTY KID FROM A FEW YEARS AGO
WHO ACCIDENTALLY TROD ON GRAHAME'S FOOT?*'

'*NO,*' said Didi, eyes wide with terror.

'*NO,*' said Hatechi, starting to shake.

'*NO, NO ONE DOES,*' Miss Firey whispered.

And so frightened were Didi and Hatechi by everything that Miss Firey had said that they did something extremely out of character. They fell to their knees and begged her not to tell, tears streaming down their faces as they rasped and heaved for breath.

This extremely convincing scene could fool many a teacher, but not the headteacher of Elemental Springs Elementary. Miss Firey knew full well that Didi could influence water, including tears, and Hatechi could influence air, so gasping for breath could be made to look like a tragic scene from the famous playwright, Throwspear. So she sat back and waited for their performance to end, a vicious grin spreading across her face.

'PERHAPS THERE IS AN ARRANGEMENT WE COULD COME TO,' Miss Firey began.

'WHAT IS IT?' asked Hatechi and Didi, turning off their theatrics like a tap.

'WELL, I'VE HAD ENOUGH OF BEING HEADTEACHER OF ELEMENTAL SPRINGS ELEMENTARY. I WANT TO TEACH AT THE ALL—ARTISTRY TEMPLE. I WANT TO WALK THE HALLOWED HALLS OF THE FIRE DIVISION AND HAVE MY NAME ETCHED ON THE BURNING PLINTH ALONG WITH ALL THE GREATS.'

'BUT WHAT'S THAT GOT TO DO WITH US?' asked Didi.

Chapter 9

WHAT IT HAD TO DO WITH THEM

Miss Firey opened the drawer in her desk and pulled out a book with a dragon-scale cover. Then she held out her hand, and a gust of flames shot the book across the room, leaving it on the table in front of Hatechi and Didi.

'OPEN IT TO PAGE SIX,' Miss Firey said.

Neither Hatechi nor Didi moved.

'WHAT ARE YOU WAITING FOR?' demanded Miss Firey.

'ER, FOR THE BOOK TO COOL DOWN,' Didi replied.

'*THEY'RE REAL DRAGON SCALES FROM ONATHORN, WHO HAS BEEN KNOWN TO SLEEP IN VOLCANOS,*' said Miss Firey. '*IT WOULD TAKE MORE THAN A FEW FLAMES TO HEAT IT. **NOW, PICK THE BOOK UP.**'*

Hatechi did as he was told. Page six was a large illustration of a grey and brown dragon.

They both looked back at their teacher in confusion.

'*THAT'S THE GUMBO DRAGON! OBVIOUSLY!*' Miss Firey spat in annoyance.

'*WE KNOW THAT,*' said Didi. '*BUT WHAT'S A MISSING DRAGON GOT TO DO WITH ANYTHING?*'

Miss Firey's eyes narrowed and then she exhaled purposefully.

ARTISTRY	99	STRENGTH	86
CUTENESS	39	CUNNING	12

ONATHORN

COURAGE	87	WISDOM	50
SPEED	69	UNIQUE POWERS	71

ONATHORN cuts a formidable figure with his imposing size and stature. Possessing the unique ability to produce fire, he stands as the only dragon with such a talent. Moreover, he is impervious to flames. Though he is a nimble flyer, he steers clear of water.

THE CIRCLE OF DRAGONS
ONATHORN CAN BEAT SWIFT. HOWEVER, IT IS QUIETSCH
WHO CAN TRIUMPH OVER ONATHORN IN BATTLE.

'DO YOU KNOW WHO WAS IN THE CROWD YESTERDAY AT THE
ELEMENTAL GAMES?'

'SOME OF THEM, I GUESS,' said Didi.

'I HAD AN OLD FRIEND THERE,' said Hatechi. 'I DON'T KNOW
HIM THAT WELL ANY MORE. WHEN WE WERE YOUNG, HE ACCUSED ME
OF NEVER LISTENING TO HIM. AT LEAST, I THINK THAT'S WHAT
HE SAID. I WASN'T PAYING ATTENTION.'

'**NO! I DIDN'T MEAN, DID YOU KNOW ANYONE IN THE
CROWD. OF COURSE YOU WOULD KNOW SOMEONE. NO!
I WAS OBVIOUSLY TALKING ABOUT SOMEONE SPECIFIC,
YOU MUDDLEHEADS!**' explained an exasperated
Miss Firey as flames whipped around her palms.
'IN THE CROWD YESTERDAY WAS A DIPLOMATIC GUEST OF PROFESSOR
BLOWPUFF. THIS GUEST IS AN EXTREMELY POWERFUL AND
DANGEROUS MAN BY THE NAME OF LORD SINGE!'

'LORD SINGE!' Hatechi and Didi gasped.

'YES, LORD SINGE!' said Miss Firey.

ARTISTRY	7	STRENGTH	17
CUTENESS	39	CUNNING	68

ROBBING ROBIN

COURAGE	28	WISDOM	13
SPEED	53	UNIQUE POWERS	59

In the shadowy corners, where darkness and danger lurk, there exists a band of mischievous tricksters known as the **ROBBING ROBINS**, or as some call them, Naughty Ninjas. These pint-sized perpetrators are possessed with cunning and agility, enabling them to slip through crevices without making a sound.

'WHO'S LORD SINGE?' Hatechi and Didi asked.

'ARE YOU TWO SERIOUS?' asked a dubious Miss Firey. 'HOW CAN YOU NOT KNOW WHO HE IS? LORD SINGE IS SUCH A POWERFUL READER THAT HE ONCE CONTROLLED TEN ROBBING ROBINS AT ONCE!'

WAIT A DRAGON DARN MINUTE!

COULD IT BE THAT CHAP YOU SAW BACK ON PAGE 61?

COULD IT BE A COINCIDENCE THAT THERE ARE ANIMALS HERE?

IF YOU WANT TO KNOW WHO IT IS

ZOOMY

ZOOM TO PAGE 151

'STUPENDOUS. OK, SO HE'S A READER, WHICH MEANS HE CAN CONTROL ANIMALS!' said Hatechi.

'BUT WHAT'S THAT GOT TO DO WITH THE GUMBO DRAGON AND US?' asked Didi.

Miss Firey squeezed her hands into two fists and leant forward on her table. 'IF I HAD THE ABILITY TO SENSE AND CONTROL ANIMALS, THAT DISGUSTING GIANT SLUG THING OF YOURS WOULD ALREADY BE UNDER MY CONTROL. THERE CAN BE ONLY ONE REASON WHY LORD SINGE HASN'T ALREADY MADE THAT CREATURE HIS PET YET.'

Didi and Hatechi looked at each other with confusion and concern.

Miss Firey continued.

'AND THAT'S BECAUSE LORD SINGE HAD NO IDEA THAT IT WAS THERE.'

Miss Firey's golden eyes flickered and narrowed. 'AND DO YOU KNOW WHY?'

Didi and Hatechi shrugged. The room was silent.

Miss Firey was still until her eyes shifted to the book on the table.

'BECAUSE THAT SLUG OF YOURS IS A DRAGON!'

she said triumphantly.

Chapter 10

Miss Firey's office was as quiet as an empty cave until Hatechi and Didi erupted in laughter.

'*A DRAGON,*' Didi giggled.

'*SHERBERT?*' Hatechi laughed. '*NO WAY!*'

'**MUDDLEHEADS!**' Miss Firey screamed, sending a fireball up across the ceiling. '*THAT GIANT SLUG OF YOURS MUST HAVE UNDERGONE SOME WEIRD MUTATION OR SPELL, BUT IT CAN ONLY BE THE GUMBO DRAGON.*'

It was then that Hatechi and Didi realised Miss Firey was serious. Hatechi looked to Didi who was already looking at him, her eyes wide with amazement. Together they slowly craned their necks towards the book. Hatechi mouthed the word 'STUPENDOUS'. Didi let out a gasp.

'SHERBERT'S A DRAGON?!'

'CORRECT. ALTHOUGH IT'S CLEARLY NOT AT THE HEIGHT OF ITS POWERS RIGHT NOW, AND THAT'S A GOOD THING!' said Miss Firey.

'WHY?' Didi asked, taking a closer look at the illustration in the book.

'BECAUSE YOU TWO CLOWNS COULDN'T POSSIBLY CONTROL A FULLY FLEDGED DRAGON! BUT FOR SOME REASON, YOU DO SEEM ABLE TO CONTROL WHATEVER IT CURRENTLY IS.'

ARTISTRY	99	STRENGTH	23
CUTENESS	48	CUNNING	26

SWIFT

COURAGE	87	WISDOM	71
SPEED	97	UNIQUE POWERS	76

SWIFT breathes out highly pressurised air that can knock anything from the skies. Swift is the fastest of all the dragons and, over short distances, she can even swim faster than Quietsch the Water Dragon. Swift gets on well with Onathorn, which is lucky, because the Fire Dragon's scorching flames are the only thing that can harm Swift.

THE CIRCLE OF DRAGONS
SWIFT CAN DEFEAT RJUKA.
ONATHORN CAN DEFEAT SWIFT.

Hatechi and Didi looked at each other, then back at Miss Firey.

'SO, WHAT IS IT YOU WANT US TO DO?'

Miss Firey took a long and satisfying inhale. She then smirked so much that her eyes looked as if they might pop out.

'PROFESSOR BLOWPUFF WAS ONCE THE GRAND MASTER OF BOING BOING AND, AS SUCH, WAS THE READER AND LINKED TO SWIFT, THE AIR DRAGON,' she began. 'AFTER BEING DEPOSED AND REPLACED AS GRAND MASTER, HE LOST THE ABILITY TO SWAY, INFLUENCE OR SENSE ANY DRAGON. SO, IF YOU GET YOUR NEW PET TO ATTACK BLOWPUFF, LITTLE OL' ME CAN COME TO THE RESCUE. ONCE I'M THE SAVIOUR OF PROFESSOR BLOWPUFF AND, THEREFORE, THE SAVIOUR OF THE ALL—ARTISTRY TEMPLE, THEY'LL FINALLY MOVE ME OUT OF ELEMENTAL SPRINGS ELEMENTARY AND PUT ME WHERE I BELONG — IN **THE TEMPLE**.'

'BUT SHERBERT WON'T ATTACK PROFESSOR BLOWPUFF,' said Didi.

'*HE DOESN'T HAVE TO. HE JUST NEEDS TO PRETEND TO. I'LL JUMP IN JUST IN THE NICK OF TIME.*' Miss Firey's golden eyes gleamed with wicked amusement. '*EITHER THAT, OR I TELL THE ENTIRE SCHOOL ABOUT YOUR SECRET AND HOW YOU WON AT THE GAMES!*'

Hatechi and Didi gasped. '*YOU KNOW ABOUT OUR SECRET?*'

Miss Firey buried her face in her palms.

'**OBVIOUSLY! WE WOULDN'T BE HAVING THIS CONVERSATION IF I DIDN'T KNOW ABOUT YOUR GIANT PET SLUG! HAVE YOU NOT LISTENED TO A WORD I'VE SAID?**'

Didi and Hatechi breathed a concealed sigh of relief.

'*WE'RE JUST JOKING WITH YOU,*' assured Hatechi.

Didi interjected. '*DON'T WORRY, MISS, WE UNDERSTOOD EVERY WORD, RIGHT HATECHI?*'

'**BIG TIME.** *UNDERSTOOD EVERY WORD, EXCEPT PERHAPS FOR ONE —* **MISDEMEANOURS.** *IS THAT A NEW TEACHER?*'

| ARTISTRY | 45 | STRENGTH | 22 |
| CUTENESS | 35 | CUNNING | 69 |

Miss D Meanours

| COURAGE | 32 | WISDOM | 76 |
| SPEED | 52 | UNIQUE POWERS | 81 |

There are numerous varieties of Wood Pixie, each
distinguished by their unique appearance and abilities.
Among them, **MISS D MEANOURS** stands out as
a Swamp Pixie from Willowhollowshire, a captivating realm
nestled within the North Woodlands Of Many Names. She
brings a touch of wild magic to the wetlands through an
ancient art called Welding. Welding is an extraordinary
practice that combines elements to craft formidable
weapons. It is worth noting that Swamp Pixies harbour
a deep disdain for Tomb Pixies.

The remainder of school that day was the weirdest ever. Hatechi and Didi kept catching Miss Firey nodding at them through the classroom window, winking at them in the cafeteria, saying '*HI*' to them in the corridor, and waving at them in the playground.

'**THIS HAS TO STOP**,' said Hatechi. '*WE LOOK LIKE WE'VE GOT SOME DEAL GOING WITH THE HEADTEACHER.*'

'*WE DO!*' said Didi.

Hatechi huffed.

'*ALL THE HARD WORK WE'VE PUT INTO BEING THE STUPENDOUS ONES IS EVAPORATING IN FRONT OF OUR EYES.*'

'*WHAT HARD WORK?*' asked Didi.

'*WELL, FOR STARTERS, THAT STRUT YOU PUT ON AND THE FAKE HEAD BOB I DO.*'

'**I DON'T PUT ON A STRUT!**'

'*SURE, YOU DO. YOUR SWAGGER IS THE REASON I INVENTED THE NONCHALANT NOD,*' Hatechi said, his bouncy hair jumping forward, then back.

'THE NONCHALANT NOD!? DO YOU MEAN YOU ACTUALLY
DO THAT ON PURPOSE? **AND I DON'T PURPOSELY SWAGGER!
I HAVE WEBBED FEET!**'

'OH,' said Hatechi. 'WELL, MAYBE WE DON'T NEED TO WORRY
TOO MUCH ABOUT BEING THE STUPENDOUS ONES THEN.'

'**LISTEN,**' said Didi. 'THERE IS ONLY ONE THING STANDING
BETWEEN THE ALL-ARTISTRY TEMPLE AND US: MISS FIREY.
SO I GUESS THE SOONER WE GET SHERBERT TO HELP HER,
THE BETTER!'

Chapter 11

The Other Thing Standing In Their Way To The All-Artistry Temple

After school that day, Hatechi and Didi **RUSHED** to their secret hideout. They realised it wasn't so secret after all when they found an unexpected visitor waiting for them.

'**GRAHAME GILLBERTHAIR!**' they screamed.

'*WHAT ARE YOU DOING HERE?*'

'WELL, I'M NOT PLAYING WITH YOUR COLLECTION OF ARTISTRY ECLIPSE CARDS, THAT'S FOR SURE! I'M HERE BECAUSE I KNOW HOW YOU WON AT THE ELEMENTAL GAMES! **I KNOW YOU CHEATED!**' Grahame replied.

Hatechi, believing that they might be about to meet a sticky end at the hands of Grahame the Executioner, grabbed Didi and gave her their coded wink.

She nodded.

'LET'S DO THIS!' Didi boomed.

They stood up straight, puffed their chests out and held their hands out in front of them. Didi began circling her arms and then the pair of them started to unleash their Artistry at full velocity.

Grahame arched an eyebrow in confusion.

'**WHAT ON ALEGNA ARE YOU DOING?**' he said.

An eerie silence filled the air for several tense seconds before three droplets of water floated from the pond into the tree house and hovered before Didi.

Hatechi followed suit, circling his arms to use his Air Artistry to send the water droplets rushing towards Grahame. However, they quickly lost momentum and trickled down before splashing harmlessly at Grahame's feet.

'*PATHETIC,*' Grahame scoffed, clearly unimpressed by their lacklustre display.

'*PLEASE DON'T KILL US!*' cried Didi.

'**WE'RE TOO YOUNG TO DIE!**'

Chapter 12

The atmosphere in the tree house was as dense as the sludgy custard in the school's cafeteria. Grahame's chuckle pierced through the thick tension.

'KILL YOU? I'M NOT GOING TO KILL YOU,' he laughed.

Didi and Hatechi breathed a sigh of relief, but their joy was short-lived. Grahame paused, his eyes glinting mischievously.

'ON SECOND THOUGHTS. MAYBE I WILL!'

Hatechi instinctively clutched Didi, holding her close. Grahame's smirk grew wider. 'BUT THEN AGAIN,

PERHAPS I'LL SPARE YOU IF YOU DO SOMETHING FOR ME.'

Hatechi's voice shook with fear as he blurted out,

'WE'LL DO ANYTHING YOU ASK!'

A wicked grin spread across Grahame's face as

he leaned in closer, his voice low and menacing.

'We will be taking that creature of yours to

the Graveyard of Sacred Sorrows.'

'FIRSTLY!' spluttered Didi,

'THAT SOUNDS TERRIFYING.

SECONDLY,' she

paused, 'ACTUALLY,

I DON'T HAVE A SECONDLY.'

'**I DO**,' Hatechi interjected, '*WHY ARE WE TAKING SHERBERT TO THE GRAVEYARD OF SACRED SORROWS?*'

Grahame rose. His head and shoulders squashed up against the low ceiling.

'*DO YOU KNOW WHY THE GUMBOS ARE NOT RESPECTED? WHY WE'RE LOOKED DOWN UPON BY THE OTHER ARTISTRY NATIONS?*' he asked.

'*BECAUSE YOU'RE ALWAYS COVERED IN MUD?*' said Didi.

'*BECAUSE YOU DON'T LIKE WEARING CLOTHES?*' said Hatechi.

'*BECAUSE YOU HAVE TERRIBLE TABLE MANNERS?*'

'*BECAUSE YOU—*'

'**NO!**' blasted Grahame. 'WE'RE LOOKED DOWN ON BECAUSE WE'RE THE ONLY ARTISTRY NATION THAT CURRENTLY DOESN'T HAVE A DRAGON. BUT YOU TWO CAN HELP ME FIX THAT. YOU'RE GOING TO BRING SHERBERT TO THE GRAVEYARD OF SACRED SORROWS WITH ME, WHERE WE SHALL RESURRECT HIM AS THE LEGENDARY GUMBO DRAGON.

I SHALL BE THE HERO OF THE GUMBO REALM, ETCHED FOREVER IN THE RECORDS OF OUR GREAT NATION'S HISTORY,' said Grahame with a sly smile.

'AND REMEMBER, IF YOU DON'T HELP ME, I'LL HAVE NO QUALMS ABOUT ENDING YOUR LIVES.'

And with that, he **LEAPT** out of the window and slid down a mudslide that fell away behind him as he yelled '**WE LEAVE NOW!**'

Hatechi turned to Didi. *'WHAT ARE WE GOING TO DO?'*

'**WE HAVE NO CHOICE.** *GRAHAME SAID HE'LL KILL US!*'

'BUT WHAT IF HE HAS IT ALL WRONG? WHAT IF SHERBERT IS JUST, WELL, SHERBERT?' asked Hatechi.

'OR WHAT IF SHERBERT IS THE GUMBO DRAGON AND DOESN'T WANT TO BE TURNED BACK?' said Didi.

'IF SHERBERT IS TURNED BACK INTO THE GUMBO DRAGON, THEN WE WON'T BE ABLE TO HELP MISS FIREY, SO WE CAN KISS GOODBYE TO GETTING INTO THE ALL—ARTISTRY TEMPLE,' Hatechi noted.

'**CORRECT!** BUT IF GRAHAME KILLS US, WE ALSO WON'T BE GOING TO THE ALL—ARTISTRY TEMPLE NEXT YEAR,' Didi replied. 'IT'S A **LOSE-LOSE** SITUATION.'

WAIT! YEP. I THINK YEP! I DO! YEP. I. I HAVE AN IDEA!

'GOOD POINT!' Hatechi said. Then he froze, his face slowly scrunching up as he stared at the ceiling.

'YOU OK?' asked Didi.

'I THINK I HAVE AN IDEA,' replied Hatechi, his forehead crunching up so much that his eyes were bobbling around.

'**WELL?** SPIT IT OUT, THEN,' said Didi.

'YEP! I HAVE AN IDEA. ONLY ONE OF US SHOULD GO TO THE GRAVEYARD OF SACRED SORROWS,' said Hatechi.

'WHAT? WHY? IF YOU THINK I WILL GO ON MY OWN WITH GRAHAME THE EXECUTIONER TO A PLACE CALLED THE GRAVEYARD OF SACRED SORROWS, THEN YOU CAN THINK AGAIN!' Didi exclaimed.

'OK. THEN YOU GO AND GET THE BACKUP,' said Hatechi.

'BACKUP? WE CAN'T TELL ANYONE ELSE ABOUT SHERBERT!'

'WE WON'T. WE'LL GET SOMEONE WHO ALREADY KNOWS,' said Hatechi with a knowing smile. 'SOMEONE WHO NEEDS SHERBERT AS HE IS. GO AND GET MISS FIREY.'

'MISS FIREY!?' Didi paused and pondered her situation. 'MAYBE THE GRAVEYARD OF SACRED SORROWS WITH GRAHAME DOESN'T SOUND SO BAD. AT LEAST I'LL BE WITH SHERBERT.'

'IT'S A PLAN THEN,' said Hatechi as he made his way to the secret exit of the tree house. 'YOU SLOW GRAHAME DOWN SO THAT MISS FIREY AND I CAN CATCH YOU UP!'

Grahame then shouted 'GET A MOVE ON YOU TWO!' from below the tree house.

Didi lightly pushed Hatechi. 'QUICK, GO. I ALREADY HAVE A PLAN FOR HOW TO SLOW HIM DOWN,' she said.

Chapter 13

The day's warmth was ebbing away, leaving the Forest of Smiles in a shroud of cool tranquillity. **KNOCK SCRAPE KNOCK**. Rodents scampered to their burrows, birds took refuge on higher branches, and deer bounded away in every direction. **KNOCK SCRAPE KNOCK**.

The sound grew closer, and soon, a creature appeared, unlike any that had ever been seen in the forest. It had white fur with matted patches of black, a bit like if a Polar Bearath had been wrestling with a Giant Ink Squid.

| ARTISTRY | 11 | STRENGTH | 91 |
| CUTENESS | 69 | CUNNING | 10 |

POLAR BEARATH

| COURAGE | 79 | WISDOM | 16 |
| SPEED | 21 | UNIQUE POWERS | 21 |

The Polar Bearath resides mostly in the far north of both the Smoke Realm and Boing Boing.
It is a gentle giant, renowned for its serene disposition and tranquil nature, yet it harbours a fierce enmity towards a certain foe - the dreaded Gorillath.

In the murky depths beyond the Barrier Serpentine, the Giant Ink Squid dwells, its massive form shrouded in mystery. Legend has it that when it emerges from the abyss, it drags ships down with it into the fathomless depths, never to be seen again.

| ARTISTRY | 56 | STRENGTH | 57 |
| CUTENESS | 59 | CUNNING | 37 |

GIANT INK SQUID

| COURAGE | 36 | WISDOM | 79 |
| SPEED | 41 | UNIQUE POWERS | 66 |

Although it *COULDN'T* have been a Polar Bearath because they don't have long blond highlighted hair. This creature also had four heavy brown sticky legs that swung, **KNOCKING** and *SCRAPING* on the rocks underneath. Not sticky in an adhesive sense. Sticky, as in, like, sticks. Because they were, in fact, thick sticks. Undoubtedly, this was a rare and exotic creature, but as you may have guessed, it was actually **SHERBERT IN DISGUISE!**

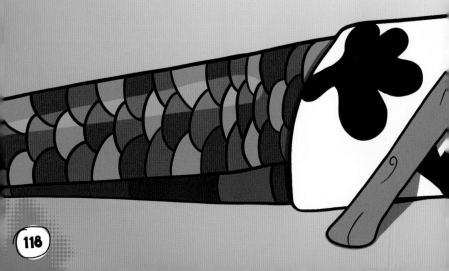

Didi's plan had been to insist that Sherbert couldn't travel without a disguise, meaning valuable time was taken up by Grahame acquiring an old cowbear skin he'd taken from the floor in the school library, a wig his mum used for special occasions, and sticks for legs. And although Sherbert's new fringe meant he occasionally bumped into a tree, and his stick legs scraped and bounced, which ruined his usual slithering stealth, Sherbert seemed to enjoy being incognito.

'*YOU LOOK RIDICULOUS,*' said Didi as she rubbed Sherbert affectionately under the chin.

And in reply, Sherbert **SHOOK** as if laughing and **wiggled** his long serpent-like body to make his rear 'legs' bounce about.

They had been creeping through the woods for thirty minutes when Grahame announced that the Gumbo town known as Bottle Neck Crush was around the next corner.

| ARTISTRY | 51 | STRENGTH | 10 |
| CUTENESS | 19 | CUNNING | 71 |

CLICKING CROW

| COURAGE | 14 | WISDOM | 79 |
| SPEED | 53 | UNIQUE POWERS | 84 |

The **CLICKING CROW** has the unique ability to read minds. yet this wondrous power remains unknown to all except the crow.

UNWELCOME TO
BOTTLE NECK
CRUSH

ZOOMY

ZOOM TO PAGE 131

123

Bottle Neck Crush had hardened mud alleys with oily puddles that weaved past compacted buildings. In the few windows where the shutters were not fastened you'd find a **Clicking Crow** making **clicking** noises when anyone got too close. No road was wide or straight as if to conceal the town's secrets, and although no building was taller than a single storey, they were bunched together in such a way that you were forever in shadow. The trio had no choice but to travel through this sinister town because there was no way around it. On either side were the Dead Wastes, once patrolled by the terrible **GORGELLA**.

| ARTISTRY | 61 | STRENGTH | 79 |
| CUTENESS | 0 | CUNNING | 84 |

GORGELLA

| COURAGE | 19 | WISDOM | 23 |
| SPEED | 41 | UNIQUE POWERS | 76 |

It is believed that the **GORGELLA** was created by a spell. In the past, wherever the Gorgella went, it brought nothing but destruction and devastation, leaving behind barren wastelands devoid of all life across the Gumbo Realm. But with the Mud Dragon's intervention, the Gorgella was finally banished, never to wreak havoc again.

'*THIS TOWN IS A BIT SMELLY,*' complained Didi.

'*I KNOW! IT'S LOVELY, ISN'T IT?*' Grahame replied.

Etched upon one of the buildings in bold, defiant letters was graffiti that read, **THE G-SMOKES RULE.**

'*WHAT ARE THE G-SMOKES?*' asked Didi.

'*A GANG OF FANATICS THAT GIVE GUMBOS A BAD NAME,*' replied Grahame. '*RUMOUR HAS IT THAT THEY WANT TO HELP EMPEROR SMOKE **DESTROY** ALL THE DRAGONS.*'

'**KILL THE DRAGONS? THAT'S IMPOSSIBLE!**' said Didi.

'**IS IT THOUGH?**' queried Grahame. '*ACCORDING TO THE CIRCLE OF DRAGONS, ONLY THE GUMBO DRAGON IS INDESTRUCTIBLE.*'

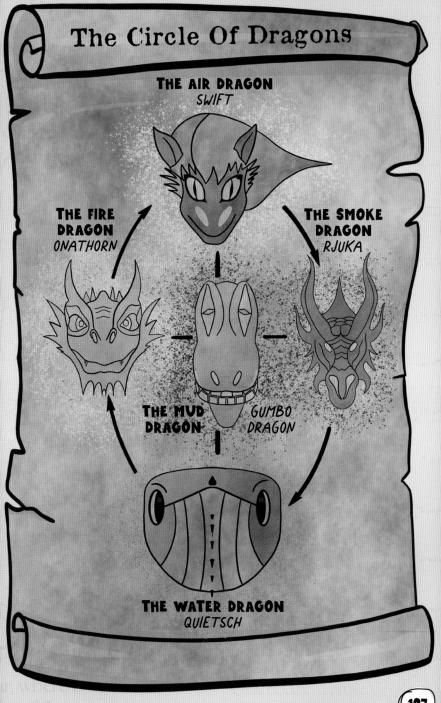

The Circle Of Dragons

THE AIR DRAGON
SWIFT

THE FIRE DRAGON
ONATHORN

THE SMOKE DRAGON
RJUKA

THE MUD DRAGON *GUMBO DRAGON*

THE WATER DRAGON
QUIETSCH

'**OI!** QUIETSCH THE WATER DRAGON CAN ONLY BE DEFEATED BY RJUKA THE SMOKE DRAGON AND RJUKA WOULDN'T DARE DO THAT BECAUSE SWIFT THE AIR DRAGON WOULD THEN BE ALLOWED TO DESTROY RJUKA,' Didi said.

'AHH, YES, BUT WHAT IF EMPEROR SMOKE FOUND A WAY TO ERADICATE SWIFT. RJUKA COULD THEN DESTROY ALL THE DRAGONS. APART FROM THE GUMBO DRAGON, OF COURSE,' scoffed Grahame.

Then his eyes narrowed as he came to a realisation. First, he stared at the graffiti, then muttered under his breath. 'IF THAT HAPPENED, THE GUMBO REALM WOULD BE THE ONLY SAFE HAVEN FROM RJUKA AND EMPEROR SMOKE, MAKING IT THE SECOND MOST POWERFUL REALM IN ALEGNA.'

ARTISTRY	99	STRENGTH	86
CUTENESS	76	CUNNING	13

QUIETSCH

COURAGE	79	WISDOM	53
SPEED	63	UNIQUE POWERS	62

QUIETSCH, which is pronounced Creetch, is the biggest of all the dragons. She has the ability to carry vast amounts of water which she can then use to flood her enemies. She's slow in the air but spends most of her time in the water.

THE CIRCLE OF DRAGONS

QUIETSCH CAN BEAT ONATHORN THE FIRE DRAGON.

RJUKA THE SMOKE DRAGON CAN BEAT QUIETSCH.

Grahame turned slowly to Sherbert, who was staring blankly ahead, his tongue lolling out of his oversized mouth, shimmering brown saliva dripping from it and landing on the ground. Then he **BELCHED** unceremoniously! He looked anything but indestructible.

Just then, a scream echoed from a nearby alleyway.

'HELP! HELP ME!' a voice yelled.

Sherbert c r a n e d his long neck in the direction of the pleading.

Didi froze.

'WHAT SHALL WE DO?' she asked.

'NOTHING!' Grahame snapped. *'WE NEED TO GET TO THE GRAVEYARD OF SACRED SORROWS!'*

ZOOMYED FROM PAGE 123

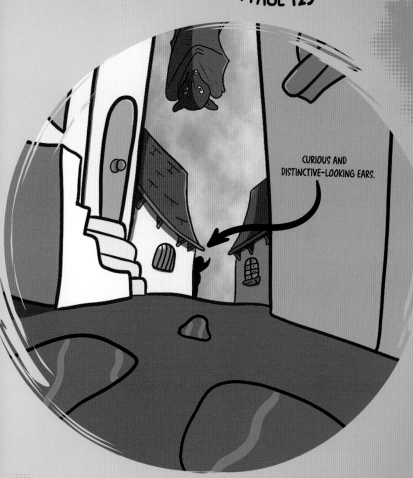

'HELP! PLEASE, HELP ME!' the voice yelled again.

Sherbert rushed to Didi and slithered around her, whimpering and trying to push her towards the distressed voice.

'FIRST, WE HELP,' Didi said.

Sherbert nodded his head frantically in agreement and slid off towards the screams.

Grahame and Didi gave chase down a tight alley. Sharp corner after sharp corner meant that Sherbert was soon out of sight. Didi tried to run faster, but the hard, compacted mud underfoot became soft and slippery. Grahame Gillberthair's wide claw-like feet gripped each corner as Didi lost her footing. She was falling behind. Another scream echoed from up ahead. Didi took off her sandals and, thanks to her slightly webbed feet, soon caught up with Grahame, who was waiting at a crossroads.

'NOT JUST USEFUL FOR SWIMMING!' Grahame smiled while pointing at Didi's feet.

'*I GUESS NOT,*' said Didi, desperately looking around for Sherbert.

She soon spotted a clue. Slime!

They rushed off, following the trail of slime, and were confident they were going the correct way when they heard the voice again. This time it was just around the next corner.

Didi sprinted off.

'**WAIT!**' warned Grahame but Didi didn't listen.

A Firey End

As Didi rounded the corner into a damp, dark, shadowy opening that stank of rotting mushrooms, at first she saw nothing. Then, the slightest of movements came from deep in the shadows. Didi's eyes adjusted to the gloom, and she inhaled sharply when she noticed three figures looming out of the darkness.

Didi gasped.

Standing in front of her, and now Grahame too, were three female Gumbos that were so huge they made Grahame look like a child. Which made sense because he was. One of the Goliath Gumbos wore a T-shirt emblazoned with **BAD TO THE BONE**. Another read **FIGHTER NOT A LOVER**. And the largest, who stood in the centre, wore a T-shirt with the dreaded word, **G-SMOKES**.

'**HELP! HELP!**' the biggest Gumbo feigned, and all three began to laugh.

The largest Gumbo then raised her hand, prompting the other two to stop laughing instantly. One of them asked, *'WHAT ARE YOU GOING TO DO, MAGGIE?'*

Maggie took a sweeping step forward and looked Didi up and down. *'AND WHAT DO WE HAVE HERE? A LITTLE WATER DANCER?* **AND WHAT ON ALEGNA IS THIS?'**

Out of the gloom emerged a mighty Gorillath, its shaggy coat of matted grey unable to mask its brawny physique. Its forearms resembled sturdy tree trunks, and its mammoth hands appeared capable of crushing stone into dust. With one of these immense hands, the Gorillath clutched Sherbert by the neck, rendering the poor creature powerless in its grip.

| ARTISTRY | 43 | STRENGTH | 69 |
| CUTENESS | 6 | CUNNING | 61 |

G-Smokes
MAGGIE

| COURAGE | 67 | WISDOM | 13 |
| SPEED | 21 | UNIQUE POWERS | 17 |

Maggie, the head of the feared Gumbo gang, the G-smokes, is a force to be reckoned with. She boasts incredible skill in Mud Artistry and her ultimate desire is to witness the collapse of every nation in Alegna except for her own. With her impressive abilities and unwavering ambition she is a formidable adversary to all who dare to cross her path.

In the forests of Alegna roams a most ill-tempered creature. It is known as the Gorillath. With a sour disposition, and a pair of strong, brawny forearms, this beast is not one to be trifled with.

| ARTISTRY | 15 | STRENGTH | 84 |
| CUTENESS | 12 | CUNNING | 68 |

GORRILATH

| COURAGE | 39 | WISDOM | 18 |
| SPEED | 56 | UNIQUE POWERS | 17 |

Sherbert thrashed his tail, **HITTING** the Gorillath in the face. In response, the Gorillath shook him violently, and as poor Sherbert was flung up and down and side to side, his long wig fell off. Then, his fake stick legs crashed to the floor.

'**SHERBERT!**' Didi shouted.

Grahame circled his arms, but before he could summon his Mud Artistry, the three Gumbos had coved *him* in thick mud.

'*NOW THEN,*' said Maggie, turning back to Didi, '*WHO ARE YOU? AND MORE IMPORTANTLY,* **WHAT'S THAT CREATURE?**' Didi could not think of anything to say, let alone a plan to get her and Sherbert out of this. Sherbert seemed to have lost consciousness in the Gorillath's grip, and the three Gumbos were snarling at Didi.

'*WELL,*' said, Maggie, '*THE IDENTITY OF THIS CREATURE MUST BE IMPORTANT IF YOU WENT TO THE TROUBLE TO DISGUISE IT.*'

Sherbert then squirmed but couldn't escape the Gorillath's grip. At least he was conscious.

Sweat dripped from Didi's forehead. Her palms were clammy. Her entire body was hot, irritable and itchy. Why was she so **RIDICULOUSLY** hot?

Then she heard an unmistakable voice coming from behind her. A voice she never thought she would be pleased to hear.

'*THERE ARE TWO THINGS A GORILLATH HATES AND ONE IS FIRE!*' said Miss Firey as she shot flames up into the twilight. The Gorillath **YELPED**, dropped Sherbert, and made its escape. Sherbert landed, snarled with annoyance, took a deep breath and spewed thick brown gunk in Didi's direction. The next thing Didi knew, she was in a murky protective mud dome along with Hatechi.

'HATECHI!' she gasped. 'WHAT'S HAPPENING OUT THERE?'

'I DON'T KNOW. I'M IN HERE WITH YOU!'

'GOOD POINT!' said Didi. 'DID MISS FIREY JUST SAVE US?'

'YES, AND I KNOW WE'LL NEVER HEAR THE END OF IT,' said Hatechi.

'WHAT SHE SAID WAS ANNOYINGLY STUPENDOUS TOO, "**THERE ARE TWO THINGS A GORILLATH HATES, AND ONE IS FIRE,**"' Didi repeated in a nasally Miss Firey tone.

'**I KNOW, RIGHT!?**

ALTHOUGH IT WAS A BIT MUCH. NOW HOW DO WE GET OUT OF HERE?' Hatechi asked but got no answer. 'YOU'RE THINKING OF A **STUPENDOUS** PHRASE TO SAY, AREN'T YOU?'

'**BIG TIME**,' said Didi. 'ALTHOUGH THE HEAT IS MAKING IT HARD TO CONCENTRATE.'

'YEAH, IT'S HOTTER THAN ONE OF CHEF FLAMES' THERMO TOASTIES.' Just then, mud from the roof of the cocoon began to drip. Light broke through, and soon, the cocoon became a muddy puddle around them, resembling warm gravy. Hatechi and Didi looked up to see Sherbert, Grahame and Miss Firey, flames swirling around them.

'**BLIMEY**,' said Hatechi, 'THIS WAS NOT A SIGHT I EXPECTED TO SEE WHEN I WOKE UP THIS MORNING!'

Chapter 15

THAT THING

The three large Gumbos were gone. The dank
mushroom smell remained.

'**WHAT NOW?**' asked Hatechi.

'*NOW WE GET YOU ALL BACK TO ELEMENTAL SPRINGS
ELEMENTARY BEFORE THOSE GUMBOS RETURN WITH
REINFORCEMENTS!*' replied Miss Firey.

'**NO WAY!**' said Grahame. '*THE GRAVEYARD OF SACRED
SORROWS ISN'T FAR NOW.*'

Miss Firey spun around. '*THAT THING STAYS EXACTLY
AS IT IS, GRAHAME GILLBERTHAIR!*'

'**THAT THING IS THE GUMBO DRAGON! IT'S MORE POWERFUL THAN ANYTHING YOU'VE EVER WITNESSED!**' snarled Grahame defiantly.

Miss Firey snarled back and flared her nostrils.

'**FIRSTLY!**' she spat, '*I'M FULLY AWARE OF WHAT IT IS! SECONDLY, I'VE WITNESSED QUIETSCH THE WATER DRAGON AND THE MIGHTY FIRE DRAGON ONATHORN. I EVEN ONCE SAW RJUKA AND BELIEVE YOU ME, COMPARED TO THE SMOKE DRAGON YOUR MUDSLINGING DRAGON IS NOTHING.*' Grahame's mouth dropped open.

'**NOTHING!?**' he exclaimed.

'OUR DRAGON TURNED HALF THE BARREN LANDS BACK TO LUSH HABITAT.'

'**HALF!** *EXACTLY!*' mocked Miss Firey. '*THEN HE VANISHED. HE DOESN'T EVEN WANT TO BE A DRAGON!*'

'**WELL, LET'S ASK HIM!**' Grahame snapped. He edged towards Sherbert and put on a wheedling voice as if trying to get a puppy's attention. Sherbert **BURPED** and then c r a n e d his lengthy neck but never met Grahame's gaze.

Instead, his eyes widened, and Didi and Hatechi had that awful feeling that someone – or *something* – was behind them. The next thing they saw was mud **SHOOTING OUT** of Sherbert's mouth *AGAIN*.

Chapter 16

MUD COCOON TWO

'*I'M STARTING TO GET A LITTLE TIRED OF THESE MUD COCOONS,*' groaned Didi.

Hatechi didn't answer.

'**HATECHI?**'

'**SHH!**' he hissed. '*LISTEN!*'

A scraping noise drew near, then a mighty roar resounded from outside, followed by thunderous thumps that shook the cocoon violently and fractured its top, causing two dazzling rays of light to burst through the cracks.

SCRAPE

SCRAPE
SCRAPE

'THERE'S A MONSTER OUT THERE,' whispered Hatechi.

The ruckus ceased abruptly, as if a teacher

had entered a classroom, and an eerie silence

descended.

'QUICK, LET ME STAND ON YOUR SHOULDERS AND SEE WHAT'S GOING ON,'

Didi whispered.

THUD

ROAR

'CAN YOU SEE ANYTHING?' asked Hatechi.

'SHERBERT IS BEING RESTRAINED BY TWO GORILLATHS AND MISS FIREY LOOKS TERRIFIED.'

Didi let out a gasp.

'IT'S THAT BLOKE WHO WAS AT THE STADIUM, THE ONE MISS FIREY TOLD US ABOUT.'

'LORD SINGE?' Hatechi gasped.

'YES! HE'S WALKING TOWARD SHERBERT!'

Lord Singe stared intently at Sherbert.

'MY, MY. IS THIS TRULY WHAT I BELIEVE IT IS?' he rasped before bursting into a terrible cackle.

Then he reached out and touched Sherbert, examining the slime on his hand before wiping it off on a Gorillath's fur. He snorted in disdain.

| ARTISTRY | 15 | STRENGTH | 45 |
| CUTENESS | 5 | CUNNING | 77 |

LORD SINGE

| COURAGE | 6 | WISDOM | 26 |
| SPEED | 17 | UNIQUE POWERS | 71 |

A skilled Reader can bend the will of the mightiest creatures with a mere thought. **LORD SINGE**, a Master Reader of great renown, has held sway over many creatures, commanding them with effortless ease. Alas, despite his impressive abilities, Lord Singe's heart yearns for a dragon. But his lack of Artistry, that elusive quality that sets the greatest Readers apart, means that his dream will forever remain out of reach.

'IMAGINE SLITHERING AROUND AND HIDING LIKE AN OVERSIZE SLUG WHEN YOU ARE ONE OF THE MOST POWERFUL CREATURES IN EXISTENCE!' he said, and cackled with laughter. '**AND NOW I CAN MAKE THAT POWER MINE.**'

Lord Singe turned, smoke spilling from his hood.

'*TO THE GRAVEYARD OF SACRED SORROWS,*' he roared.

'*THEY'RE LEAVING,*' said Didi, who looked over as

Sherbert was dragged away.

Just then, Sherbert squirmed, and spat

something round and shiny high into the sky.

Didi leapt off Hatechi's shoulders.

'WE NEED TO SAVE SHERBERT!' Hatechi

exclaimed. **'HE WOULDN'T HAVE LEFT US TRAPPED**

IN HERE WITH NO WAY TO ESCAPE.'

'WHAT'S THAT WHISTLING NOISE?' asked Didi, tilting her head.

'I CAN'T HEAR ANYTHING,' answered Hatechi, cupping his ear.

'IT SOUNDS LIKE A METAL DISC FLYING THROUGH THE AIR. **IT'S GETTING LOUDER**,' said Didi, her voice rising with concern.

'OH, YEAH, I HEAR IT NOW,' said Hatechi.

'**GET DOWN!**' shouted Didi.

CRASH!

Chapter 17

THAT GREAT WONDERFUL HISTORICAL SUSPENSEFUL MOMENT OF THE AMULET

Cascaded around Hatechi and Didi were shards of mud from the now broken cocoon.

'**STUPENDOUS!**' cried Hatechi.

Within these shards a glint of light sparkled in the sunlight.

Didi reached down and picked up an amulet. Then gasped when she saw the symbols that were carved into it.

'**LOOK!** *OLD SPELL SYMBOLS,*' said Didi.

'*WHAT DOES IT SAY?*' asked Hatechi.

Didi checked to make sure no one was near

then said, '*MUM TAUGHT BOTH OF US HOW TO READ OLD SPELLS.*'

'*I KNOW AND I WOULD HAVE PAID MORE ATTENTION IF*

I'D THOUGHT I'D EVER NEED IT,' said Hatechi.

Didi pulled the amulet closer, studied the

symbols and began to read:

ARTISTRY	45	STRENGTH	47
CUTENESS	51	CUNNING	79

Amulet of Power

COURAGE	32	WISDOM	89
SPEED	29	UNIQUE POWERS	78

The **AMULET OF POWER** holds the secret of transformation. If it was to fall into the wrong hands it could mean the end of civilisation in Alegna.

Part to unleash the power of transformation,
to save the spell-makers from their damnation.
For too long have they been oppressed,
their magic hidden and repressed.

But now the time has come to break free.
To reclaim their power and their destiny.
To separate from the shadows of the past.
And unleash their magic that's built to last.

But with this magic, others must beware,
for the dragons will no longer keep peace fair.
Weakened and threatened by the spell-makers' might,
they will fight back with all their power and might.

Without the Circle of Dragons' embrace,
Peace will vanish, leaving an empty space.
In Alegna's lands, where magic once flowed,
A new tale of sorrow will then be sowed.

IT'S A BIT MUCH!' said Hatechi grabbing the amulet from Didi. *'LOOK, THERE'S A JOIN DOWN THE MIDDLE.* **LET'S SEPARATE IT TO UNLEASH THE POWER!'**

'ARE YOU CRAZIER THAN A MILK-DRINKING COWY?' said Didi snatching the amulet back. *'SHERBERT SPAT IT OUT TO BREAK THE COCOON, NOT FOR US TO SEPARATE THE AMULET AND UNLEASH SOME POWER WE KNOW NOTHING ABOUT.'*

COWY

'OR MAYBE HE WANTED US TO SEPARATE IT TO HELP SAVE HIM?' argued Hatechi.

'IT'S POSSIBLE,' replied Didi as she turned the amulet over and noticed it was corroded on the edges. 'THIS IS MADE OF THE SAME SUBSTANCE MUM'S RING WAS MADE OF.'

'**STAR STONE, YOU SURE?** MUM SAID THERE WAS NONE LEFT,' Hatechi asked.

'LOOK, IT'S JUST LIKE IT.'

'YOU'RE RIGHT. **WAIT!**' Hatechi said. 'BUT THE EDGES ARE CORRODED. STAR STONE DOESN'T CORRODE.'

'NO, BUT MAYBE IT CAN BE CORRODED BY A DRAGON PARTLY DIGESTING IT?' asked Didi.

Hatechi smiled. 'SO YOU'RE TELLING ME THAT WE HAVE **A PARTLY DIGESTED AMULET OF POWER**?'

'I DON'T KNOW. BUT ANYTHING TO DO WITH OLD SPELLS MEANS IT'S PROBABLY **DANGEROUS**,' Didi said, her eyes growing with worry.

'YOU'RE RIGHT. IF WE SEPARATE THE TWO SIDES, IT COULD MEAN GAME OVER FOR US,' said Hatechi.

'*THAT WOULD BE BAD!*' Didi replied and flicked her fringe from her eyes. '*IN THAT CASE, WE SHOULD ONLY USE IT IF WE HAVE NO OTHER CHOICE, LIKE IN A* **LIFE-OR-DEATH** *SITUATION,*' said Didi.

'*LIFE—OR—DEATH SITUATION? YOU MEAN* **DEATH-OR-DEATH SITUATION**, *SURELY?*'

'*I'M PRETTY SURE THE EXPRESSION IS "LIFE—OR—DEATH",*' puzzled Didi.

Hatechi wagged his finger.

'*IF WE'RE IN A LIFE—OR—DEATH SITUATION, WE JUST CHOOSE*

LIFE. BUT IF WE FIND OURSELVES IN A DEATH—OR—DEATH SITUATION, WE'LL HAVE TO USE THE AMULET. WHICH WOULD EITHER END UP BEING A DEATH—OR—DEATH—OR—DEATH SITUATION OR A DEATH—OR—DEATH—OR—LIFE SITUATION!'

'**NOT QUITE AS CATCHY!**' said Didi. '*LET'S JUST SAVE THE AMULET AND ONLY USE IT IF WE ABSOLUTELY HAVE TO.*'

'**AGREED!**'

Didi put the amulet in her pocket and our two philosophical saviours gave chase, following the trail of SLIME that Sherbert had left.

Chapter

18

OMD

(IF YOU'RE WONDERING WHAT OMD MEANS, IT'S LIKE OMG, BUT IN A WORLD WITH DRAGONS.)

Didi and Hatechi whizzed through an echoey canyon, sprinted past ghostly shapes, and wove through a load of bones that seemed to be moving! Then, entering a graveyard, out of breath, they stopped abruptly and ducked behind a gravestone. The graveyard was surrounded by ancient leafless trees, their branches bent and

crooked and seemingly held together by
a mass of cobwebs.

The wind whistled through these branches,
creating hundreds of whispers.

Didi and Hatechi peeked out from their
hiding place.

'*THERE THEY ARE,*' whispered Hatechi.

'**OMD!**' said Didi.

'**OMD!**' said Hatechi.

Lord Singe stood tall, his eyes piercing as he
glared at Grahame and Miss Firey, who were being
held captive in front of him. He lifted his hand, and
the shackles of smoke tightened around their wrists,
making them yelp in pain. Maggie and her Gumbo
friends stood by, ready to follow his every
command, while a pair of spine-chilling
creatures lurked in the shadows,
waiting for their turn to strike.

'IT WASN'T A MONSTER THAT WE HEARD FROM THE COCOON. IT WAS A CROCAVILE AND AN INFERNO-LION,' whispered Didi, her voice barely audible.

The Inferno-Lion puffed its chest out in pride, its mane ablaze with flickering flames. The fiery light danced and cast shifting shadows on the Crocovile's fearsome face. The Crocovile, for its part, stood upright and unflinching, its scales gleaming like forged iron, a true specimen of ferocity and power.

'I THINK WE WOULD HAVE HAD MORE CHANCE AGAINST A MONSTER,' Hatechi replied, his voice full of fear.

Sherbert **YELPED** in anguish. Hatechi and Didi crouched behind the gravestone, their eyes wide with horror, as they watched their friend being violently shaken by the two monstrous Gorillaths.

'WE HAVE TO DO SOMETHING!' Didi said looking to Hatechi for inspiration. Hatechi's jaw shook and his eyes widened as he whispered.

'WHAT IS LORD SINGE DOING?'

| ARTISTRY | 16 | STRENGTH | 81 |
| CUTENESS | 16 | CUNNING | 68 |

CROCAVILE

| COURAGE | 31 | WISDOM | 17 |
| SPEED | 19 | UNIQUE POWERS | 34 |

CROCAVILES can be found in both the Gumbo Realm and Chugwater. They are renowned for their robust build and formidable jaws. They have also been known to boast that the five dragons are descended from them. This is, of course, false.

Coming from the plains of Burning Well, the **INFERNO-LION** is an impressive beast with flames rippling through its mane.

| ARTISTRY | 63 | STRENGTH | 63 |
| CUTENESS | 47 | CUNNING | 17 |

INFERNO-LION

| COURAGE | 92 | WISDOM | 46 |
| SPEED | 71 | UNIQUE POWERS | 36 |

Chapter 19

Lord Singe hovered above the ground on a wisp of smoke. His grey and black gown quivered. His gloved hands seemed to dance slowly in front of him as if conducting an evil orchestra. Smoke seeped from his hood, concealing all but his beady red eyes. The sky turned a **MENACING** shade of grey as Lord Singe sent up a plume of smoke.

Didi turned to Hatechi and asked, *'WHAT SHALL WE DO?'*

'I HAVE NO IDEA,' replied Hatechi, who was so scared that he looked like he was about to jump out of his skin. His eyes were as big as a Night & Gale owl's.

| ARTISTRY | 22 | STRENGTH | 13 |
| CUTENESS | 71 | CUNNING | 19 |

NIGHT & GALE

| COURAGE | 33 | WISDOM | 47 |
| SPEED | 57 | UNIQUE POWERS | 41 |

The **NIGHT & GALE OWL** only lives in Boing Boing. It can create a small gale behind it which thrusts it through the air. As a nocturnal creature it is rarely seen, although with its huge eyes the chances are it can see you!

'WHAT A GLORIOUS MOMENT,' Lord Singe

hissed and smoke surged into a large open grave.

'AS SOON AS THE CHAMBER OF CHANGE IS FULL OF MY SMOKE,

THE TRANSFORMATION WILL BRING BACK THE GUMBO DRAGON,

BUT WITH ONE SLIGHT IMPROVEMENT!'

'YOU CAN'T IMPROVE PERFECTION!' shouted

Grahame Gillberthair defiantly.

'MAYBE NOT, BUT I WILL BE ABLE TO CONTROL IT!'

cackled Lord Singe.

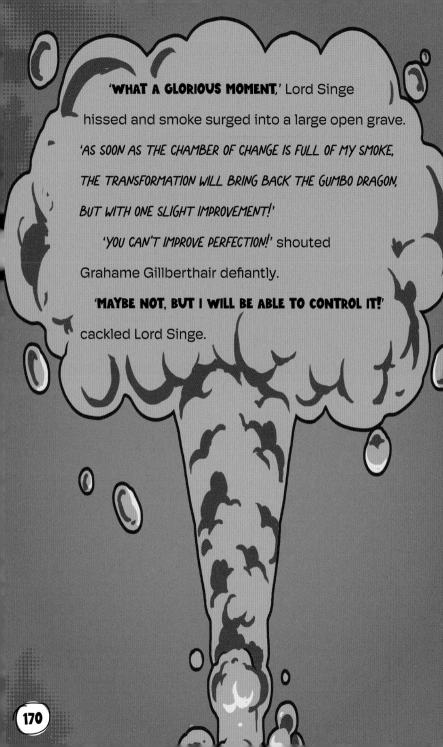

Chapter
20

Didi turned to Hatechi, who was panting furiously.

'PULL YOURSELF TOGETHER BEFORE I MAKE YOU WET YOURSELF!'

Hatechi took a little sip of air, shook his head,

clenched his fists and looked Didi directly in the eyes.

'OK,' he said.

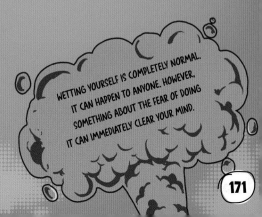

WETTING YOURSELF IS COMPLETELY NORMAL. IT CAN HAPPEN TO ANYONE. HOWEVER, SOMETHING ABOUT THE FEAR OF DOING IT CAN IMMEDIATELY CLEAR YOUR MIND.

'WE HAVE TO SAVE SHERBERT,' said Didi. 'WE CAN'T LET LORD SINGE CONTROL HIM!'

Hatechi clenched his jaw, his nostrils flared, and he grabbed his sister's hand. Didi squeezed his hand back.

'HATECHI. YOU'VE GOT THAT CRAZY LOOK IN YOUR EYE!'

Hatechi tightened his grip, let out a battle cry, and started to run towards Sherbert.

Unfortunately, running while holding hands in a graveyard was not the best idea. Hatechi and Didi fell into an empty grave with a **THUMP**!

Chapter 21

Hatechi and Didi peered up from the bottom of the empty grave, and there he was, Lord Singe. His red eyes appeared and disappeared within his smoke–filled hood. The potent smell of singed hair made their throats itch.

'**REALLY!?**' sneered Lord Singe.

'*LET OUR FRIENDS GO, YOU BIG SMOKY SMOKE, SMOKE!*' stuttered Hatechi.

Didi turned to Hatechi and raised an eyebrow.

'*SMOKY SMOKE, SMOKE?*'

'I'M NERVOUS, ALL RIGHT? *I COULDN'T THINK OF ANYTHING STUPENDOUS OR WITTY,'* he replied anxiously.

'WHAT ABOUT **"YOU SMOULDERING SOOT-FACED FOOL?"** *OR,* **"YOU DAMP BONFIRE?"** *OR,* **"YOU BURNT-OUT CHARCOAL CHEWER?"',**

'ENOUGH!' hissed Lord Singe. *'LET'S SEE HOW NOT FUNNY YOU TWO ARE WITH LUNGS FULL OF SMOKE.'*

Slivers of grey smoke began to creep into the pit. Sherbert called out for them with a whimper before being silenced by one of the two Gorillaths who were grasping him. Smoke spiralled around Hatechi's and Didi's legs, constricting with each rotation. The two gasped for air and clung to each other tightly.

'ER, I THINK WE MIGHT BE IN A DEATH—OR—DEATH—OR—DEATH SITUATION,' Hatechi gulped.

Lord Singe swooped closer.

'NOT SO FUNNY NOW, ARE YOU?' he cackled.

Chapter 22

WHAT HATECHI AND DIDI ACTUALLY DO BEST

Our two would-be heroes grasped each other as smoke gushed into the deep ditch. Hurtling haphazardly, the wisps of smoke seemed to hiss around them like a thousand **ANGRY** snakes. Hatechi reached for the amulet. Didi grabbed his hand.

'**WAIT**,' she said. '*WE CAN DO THIS!*'

'*WE CAN?*' Hatechi asked, his eyes like marbles.

'*OF COURSE, WE CAN,*' Didi said as the thick smoke reached their waists. '*LET'S DO WHAT WE DO BEST.*'

'*SLEEP?*' quizzed Hatechi.

HA HA

'**NO**,' Didi grinned. '*LORD SINGE DOESN'T THINK WE'RE FUNNY.*

SO LET'S GIVE HIM FUNNY.'

Didi swirled her index finger. Hatechi smiled knowingly, then pointed at Lord Singe.

'LOOK, EVERYONE. **LORD SINGE HAS WET HIMSELF!**'

'**WHAT?**' Lord Singe said nervously looking down at the wetness building around his robe. '**NO!** *I HAVE NOT. IT WAS THEM!*'

As Lord Singe frantically looked around at his goons, he let out an almighty fart. **FART**. He then grabbed his tummy as if cramping up, his face getting redder and redder. Then another fart ripped into the air. **FART**. One of the Gumbos let out a laugh. **FART**. It wasn't long until the whole graveyard was in tears of laughter.

'*I'M SO SORRY,*' spluttered Lord Singe. '*THIS DOESN'T NORMALLY HAPPEN.*'

Another fart echoed off the gravestones. **FART**.

Lord Singe grabbed his wet robes and swiftly rushed

off into the treeline, farting the whole way.

FART. FART. FART.

Chapter 23

Now?

Didi and Hatechi, now free of smoke, scampered out of the empty grave. As they emerged, the laughter that had filled the air was replaced with shrieks, snarls and savage growls.

'**OH NO!**' said Hatechi.

In the absence of Lord Singe, the Inferno-Lion, Crocavile and the Gorillaths had reverted to their wild ways. Maggie and the Gumbos were

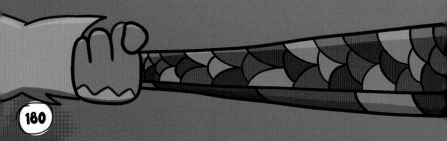

in a mad dash to escape the chaos that had erupted. Grahame Gillberthair was pinned against a gravestone, helpless as the Inferno-Lion's flaming mane flickered **DANGEROUSLY** close to him. Miss Firey **HURLED FIREBALLS** at the oncoming Crocavile, but the beast's formidable scales proved impervious to her assault. Despite her valiant efforts, the creature drew nearer, its massive jaws parting to reveal rows of gleaming teeth.

Miss Firey sank to one knee, her strength flagging under the weight of her exertions.

With each passing moment, the Crocavile drew closer, its eyes glinting with hunger and malice. Meanwhile, the two Gorillaths were engaged in a fierce **TUG-OF-WAR** over poor Sherbert, who was trapped in their relentless grasp. The hapless creature could not wriggle free, and his throat was tightly constricted by the manic Gorillath. Things were **NOT** looking good.

'**NOW?**' asked Didi desperately while holding the amulet aloft.

A subtle nod from Didi was all the encouragement Hatechi needed. With bated breath, they snapped the amulet in half, but to their dismay...

Nothing.

The terrible roaring, screaming and furious hissing continued unabated.

'**OH, PLOPS!**' Didi said.

'*IN HINDSIGHT, WE SHOULD HAVE TESTED THIS OUT FIRST,*' said Hatechi.

'**OH WAIT!**' said Didi. '*MAYBE THE PIECES NEED TO BE SEPARATED MORE.*'

Didi and Hatechi tugged on their halves of the amulet but a magnet-like force pulled the pieces back together.

'**AGAIN!**' blasted Hatechi. '**WITH ALL OUR MIGHT. AFTER THREE, PULL.**'

'*OKAY. I HOPE YOU'RE THINKING OF SOMETHING STUPENDOUS TO SAY,*' said Didi.

'*ONE, TWO,* **THREE.**'

Chapter 24

The **SCREAMS**, **ROARS** and *HISSES* that had filled the graveyard suddenly ceased, but it was far from peaceful. Instead, a deafening, thunderous screech resounded, echoing through the very bones of all those who heard it.

'**OMD!**' said Didi.

'**LITERALLY!**' said Hatechi.

The two Gorillaths were looking towards the sky, wide-eyed and frozen in fear. The Inferno-Lion seemed to have passed out. And the Crocavile was scurrying away.

ARTISTRY	99	STRENGTH	90
CUTENESS	15	CUNNING	19

GUMBO/MUD/TSL
DRAGON

COURAGE	89	WISDOM	63
SPEED	56	UNIQUE POWERS	87

The **GUMBO DRAGON'S** real name is Terragonis scutumfendens Limomucosus which is why he's referred to as the Gumbo Dragon or Mud Dragon as that's a bit of a mouthful! He can crush rocks with his powerful jaws and spits mud which he can shape into almost anything. The mud he spews is super-fertile and can change even the most barren of lands into a lush oasis. He has indestructible armour which is even resistant to all the other dragons' powers.

IN THE <u>CIRCLE OF THE DRAGONS</u> THE GUMBO DRAGON IS UNIQUE AS HE CANNOT DEFEAT ANY DRAGON OR BE DEFEATED BY ONE.

In the sky, flapping its bat-like wings, was the Gumbo Dragon. Its body was the size of an **ENORMOUS** rhinoceros with shimmering brown layers of skin that looked like welded sheets of armour. Muddy saliva dripped from its deep, wide hippopotamus-like jaw, which was full of flat teeth designed for crushing stone. Although the Gumbo Dragon looked cumbersome, it wasn't. It flitted around like a bat. Its fat, flat tail was just as much a weapon as it was a balancing device.

'BEAUTIFUL!' shouted Grahame Gillberthair.

'DISGUSTING!' yelled Miss Firey.

'STUPENDOUS!' screamed Didi and Hatechi.

The Gumbo Dragon then took a snotty inhale and, in a split second, covered the two Gorillaths with a pile of vile-smelling mud.

'OMD! *THAT SMELLS ATROCIOUS,'* said Didi holding her nose.

'*IT SMELLS LIKE A FIELD FULL OF COWYPATS!*' said Hatechi.

'*THAT'S NO* **ORDINARY MUD***!*' shouted Grahame Gillberthair.

'**YEAH, IT SMELLS LIKE —**'

'**SHHH!**' Miss Firey shouted. '*WHAT'S HAPPENING?*'

The Gumbo Dragon touched down and folded its wings. A **CRACK** came from the 'mud' pile, followed by another. A Gorillath's arm burst through the top of the magic cocoon. Clambering out, the previously grumpy grey Gorillaths had transformed into a radiant yellow, and both were beaming with gorgeous grins. Waving their hands and wiggling their fingers at the onlookers, they bounced cheerfully off into the woods.

187

ARTISTRY **16** STRENGTH **86**

CUTENESS **27** CUNNING **41**

GORILLATHY

COURAGE **39** WISDOM **18**

SPEED **49** UNIQUE POWERS **10**

Rare as a smile on Miss Firey's face, the yellow **GORILLATHY** is a creature with a remarkably sunny disposition. Its fragrance is as delicate as a meadow of spring flowers. Its forearms possess a tad more might than those of the Grey Gorillath, a trait that only serves to increase the Grey Gorillath's grouchiness.

The Gumbo Dragon let out a **ROAR**, its large tail scraping across the soil as it approached Didi and Hatechi. Its armoured plates pivoted with each thumping step.

'*SHERBERT?*' Didi said nervously.

A **BROWN GOO** dripped from the dragon's mouth as it bared its teeth.

'*THAT'S A SMILE, RIGHT?*' said Hatechi.

'*I HOPE SO!*' said Didi.

The tail of the dragon lifted with a snaking grace, swaying back and forth like a feline predator stalking its prey. A **gargling** noise came from its throat as the beast drew in a deep breath, filling its chest with air. Hatechi and Didi stood transfixed, unable to tear their gaze away from the dragon's narrowed, piercing eyes and its opening jaw.

'**OH, NO!**' Hatechi murmured, and Didi nodded in silent agreement, both anticipating being covered in another mud cocoon, this one far more foul-smelling.

'IF WE END UP YELLOW AND FLUFFY, I WON'T BE HAPPY!' said Hatechi.

SPLAT!

The dragon's mouth shot out not mud but a long chameleon-like tongue. The pink sticky tongue splodged onto each half of the

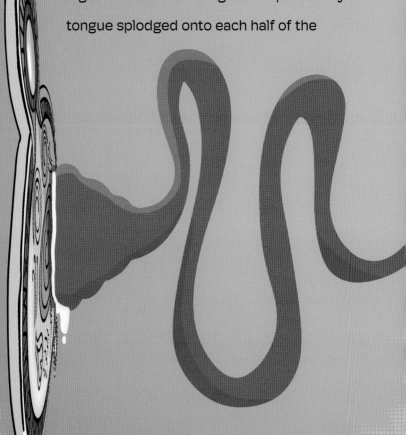

amulet, flicking them into the air.

The two halves span through the air growing closer, then **sNAP**, they connected.

'**NO!**' shouted Grahame Gillberthair as the Gumbo Dragon transformed back into Sherbert.

Back in his serpent–slug–like form Sherbert caught the twirling whole amulet in his mouth and swallowed, let out a burp and excitedly slithered around chasing his tail.

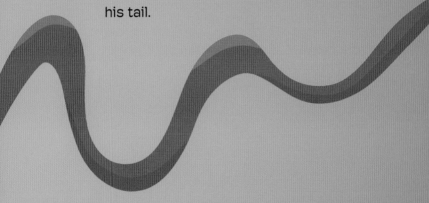

'**SHERBERT!**' Hatechi and Didi screamed with joy.

Sherbert pounced on them and began licking their faces.

'**That tickles,**' giggled Hatechi.

'*BUT YOUR BREATH SMELLS SURPRISINGLY OK,*' said Didi,
'*LIKE CHARCOAL CHOCOLATE.*'

Miss Firey snorted.

'**DISGUSTING!** *THE ONLY REASON I'M TOLERATING THIS
NAUSEATING DISPLAY IS THAT NOW WE CAN RETURN HOME AND
MAKE USE OF SHERBERT THE SLUG.*'

Didi turned to Miss Firey.

'SHERBERT HELPS YOU, AND YOU KEEP HIM A SECRET, AGREED?'

Miss Firey inhaled. '**CORRECT**,'

'EVEN IF YOUR PLAN DOESN'T END UP WITH YOU TEACHING
IN THE **ALL-ARTISTRY TEMPLE**? WE FULFIL OUR PART OF
THE BARGAIN AND YOU PROMISE NOT TO TELL ANYONE
ABOUT SHERBERT?'

Miss Firey prickled with annoyance.

'**AGREED**,'

'AND WHAT ABOUT YOU, GRAHAME?' said Hatechi.

'**WHAT NOW?**'

Grahame tilted his head to the side allowing his neck to click. *'WELL, FOR SOME OBSCURE REASON, THE MIGHTY GUMBO DRAGON PREFERS BEING —'* Grahame paused then gestured at Sherbert, *'**WHATEVER** THAT IS.'*

Sherbert swivelled and slid over to Grahame, nuzzling up to him. And in return Grahame couldn't help petting Sherbert. Then the proud Grahame Gillberthair allowed himself a giggle before continuing.

'AND FOR SOME EVEN MORE OBSCURE REASON, HE LIKES YOU TWO. SO YOUR SECRET IS SAFE WITH ME. NO ONE WOULD BELIEVE ALL THIS ANYWAY.'

Hatechi and Didi turned to each other and high-fived.

'**TO THE ALL-ARTISTRY TEMPLE, BABY!**' Hatechi said.

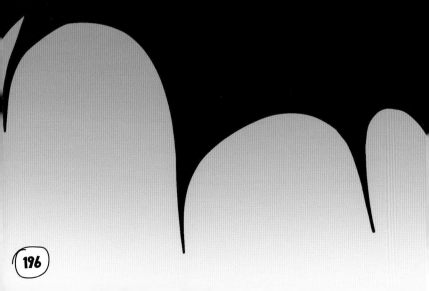

But at that moment, the rank smell of sulphur touched their nostrils. Sherbert let out a **YELP** and started to shake. Darkness descended on the graveyard. High up in the sky, an oversized silhouette with a trail of smoke eclipsed the sun. They watched in silence as an imposing dragon flew past.

Once gone, sunlight returned to the graveyard.

'**RJUKA**,' Miss Firey said, the name getting caught in her throat.

'*WE SHOULD GO*,' advised Grahame.

'**WAIT!**' Hatechi cried.

'**WHERE'S SHERBERT GONE?**'

screamed Didi.

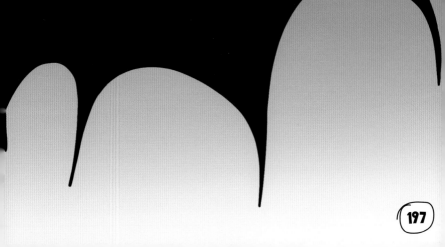

Chapter 25

THE AFTERMATH

The following day the sky was a glorious blue with a splatter of **puffy white clouds**. Nestled high on the horizon behind the Teaching Huts of Elemental Springs Elementary, the **ALL-ARTISTRY TEMPLE** looked magnificent. Our unlikely heroes, weary from their prolonged search for Sherbert, had succumbed to exhaustion. In the end, they had conceded that if Sherbert wished to be discovered, he would have done as he always did and left behind a trail of glistening slime for them to track.

'YOU KNOW WHAT ANNOYS ME THE MOST ABOUT YESTERDAY?' said Didi.

'SHERBERT'S GONE INTO HIDING?' said Hatechi.

'WELL, YES, OBVIOUSLY THAT, BUT APART FROM THAT?' replied Didi.

'WE NO LONGER HAVE A RARE AMULET OF POWER? MISS FIERY AND GRAHAME KNOW ABOUT SHERBERT? WE DIDN'T FIND OUT THE SECOND THING GORILLATHS ARE SCARED OF?'

'**YEAH, APART FROM ALL THAT,**' said Didi placing her hands on her hips. '*AFTER RECONNECTING THE AMULET, WE DIDN'T SAY ANYTHING STUPENDOUS,*' said Didi.

'**PLOPS!**' said Hatechi. '*THAT MIGHT BE WHY PEOPLE SAY THEIR STUPENDOUS LINE FIRST. OTHERWISE, THEY'LL JUST FORGET IN THE EXCITEMENT. WE SHOULD PREPARE A COUPLE OF PHRASES FOR NEXT TIME.*'

'**GOOD IDEA.** *WE COULD ADD THE WORD JUSTICE TO THE END OF THINGS. THAT MAKES EVERYTHING SOUND STUPENDOUS,*' suggested Didi.

'*IT DOES?*' quizzed Hatechi.

'*YEAH,*' said Didi. '*LISTEN. THE SHIELD OF JUSTICE. THE SWORD OF JUSTICE. IT EVEN WORKS ON WORDS LIKE TROUSERS.* **The Trousers of Justice.** *SEE.*'

'**The Flip-flops of Justice,**' Hatechi pondered. '*YOU'RE RIGHT! IT WORKS. ALTHOUGH IT'S NOT REALLY A PHRASE IS IT? I'M NOT SURE IT WOULD HAVE ADDED MUCH TO THE MOMENT*

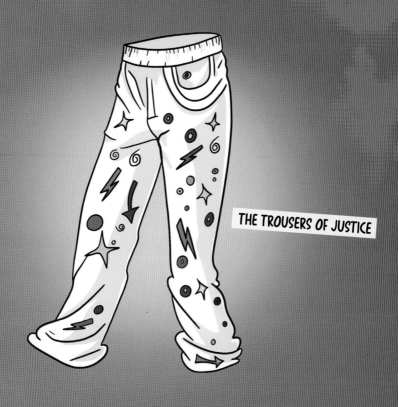

THE TROUSERS OF JUSTICE

IF, JUST BEFORE WE DETACHED THE AMULET, WE HAD YELLED,

THE TROUSERS OF JUSTICE.'

'NO, WE WOULD HAVE SAID SOMETHING LIKE, PREPARE FOR

THE AMULET OF JUSTICE. IT'S LIKE A BACKUP PLAN IF WE CAN'T

THINK OF ANYTHING. FOR EXAMPLE, YOU'RE ABOUT TO ATTACK A

MONSTER, AND YOU SCREAM, HERE COMES THE HATECHI OF JUSTICE.'

'*THERE ARE A FEW PROBLEMS WITH THAT,*' said Hatechi.

'*MAINLY BEING THE* **"ME"** *ATTACKING A MONSTER PART. SO MAYBE WE JUST LEAVE IT.*'

'*YEAH, I DOUBT ANYTHING EXCITING WILL HAPPEN TO US AGAIN ANYWAY,*' agreed Didi.

Arriving at class, our two Singe-defeating heroes discovered that Miss Firey wasn't there.

'**MISS FIREY IS UNAVAILABLE TODAY,**' said Dr Dinglebee, eyeing Hatechi and Didi with contempt. '*SHE SAYS YOU TWO HAVE TO SPEND THE DAY CLEANING THE FIRE PITS.*' Dr Dinglebee smirked while handing them each a dustpan and brush.

| ARTISTRY | 6 | STRENGTH | 17 |
| CUTENESS | 39 | CUNNING | 91 |

DR DINGLEBEE

| COURAGE | 18 | WISDOM | 71 |
| SPEED | 37 | UNIQUE POWERS | 68 |

DR DINGLEBEE is a Wood Pixie of the Tomb Pixie variety, hailing from the shadowy Whispering Warrens, situated in the south Woodlands of Many Names. The Doctor does not possess the ability to manipulate their Artistry outwards nor are they a Reader that can hold sway over the minds of beasts. Dr Dinglebee is a masterful herbalist, weaving intricate spells from the roots and leaves of the earth.

It is worth noting that Tomb Pixies harbour a deep disdain for Swamp Pixies.

Chapter 26

THE FIRE PITS

The Fire Pits was a massive room built of stone with an extremely high roof. It was where the fire students practised their Artistry and, over the years, fire had eroded away the stone floor, creating a **VAST CRATER**. It had taken Hatechi and Didi a while to get there due to it being situated on the outskirts of the Fire Divisions part of the **ALL-ARTISTRY TEMPLE**.

Burnt debris was everywhere. Hundreds of ash mounds made the **CRATER** look like it was covered in molehills, and the soot-stained walls appeared like a dirty canvas.

'**BLIMEY**,' said Hatechi standing in the doorway. '*THIS ROOM LOOKS LIKE IT'S NEVER BEEN CLEANED.*'

But, armed with their dustpans and brushes, Hatechi and Didi slowly set to work.

'YEAH, SOMETHING'S NOT RIGHT,' said Didi. 'DID YOU NOTICE THAT GRAHAME WASN'T IN CLASS, EITHER? DO YOU THINK HE'S TEAMED UP WITH MISS FIREY AND GONE TO TRY AND FIND SHERBERT?'

'**THOSE TWO! WORKING TOGETHER?**' Hatechi burst into laughter. 'THERE'S MORE CHANCE OF MISS FIREY LIVING IN A WOODEN HOUSE.' Hatechi then sighed. 'I JUST HOPE SHERBERT IS OK.'

Didi placed her hand on his shoulder.

'SHERBERT WILL COME BACK. HE'S PROBABLY JUST SLEEPING SOMEWHERE. I IMAGINE THAT CHANGING FROM SHERBERT INTO ONE OF THE MOST POWERFUL CREATURES IN ALEGNA AND BACK INTO SHERBERT AGAIN COULD BE QUITE DRAINING.'

'**I HOPE YOU'RE RIGHT**,' said Hatechi. 'HE WAS STUPENDOUSLY IMPRESSIVE AS THE GUMBO DRAGON.'

'**BIG TIME!**' Didi exclaimed.

'NOT SURE I'd CHOOSE TO BE SHERBERT IF I COULD BE AN INDESTRUCTIBLE DRAGON,' Hatechi said.

'YEAH, IT MAKES NO SENSE,' mused Didi. **THAT'S IT!** HE MUST BE TRYING TO DESTROY THE AMULET BY DIGESTING IT.'

'**YOU'RE RIGHT! HE'S TRYING TO PROTECT ALL THE DRAGONS, EVEN IF IT PUTS HIMSELF AT RISK**.'

Just then, they were cut off by a **soft** but **POWERFUL** voice.

ODD-LOOKING STATUES

Chapter 27

BLOWPUFF

Didi and Hatechi stood in the Fire Pits, open-mouthed. In front of them was a man floating just off the floor, the hem of his robes rippling as though swayed by the soft notes of a hidden lullaby. His long grey and white beard hung like a **perfect cloud**. His dragon hawk sat perched on his shoulder.

'YOU TWO SHOULD KNOW THAT NO ONE EVER CLEANS THE FIRE PITS. THE HEAT FROM THE FIRE DOES A GOOD ENOUGH JOB.'

'**PROFESSOR BLOWPUFF!**' gasped Hatechi and Didi.

| ARTISTRY | 89 | STRENGTH | 16 |
| CUTENESS | 28 | CUNNING | 50 |

BLOWPUFF

| COURAGE | 78 | WISDOM | 87 |
| SPEED | 76 | UNIQUE POWERS | 67 |

Professor Blowpuff is considered one of the most powerful Artistry wielders in Alegna. He can use Air, Water, Fire, Smoke and even Mud. He was once the Grand Master of Boing Boing and linked with the dragon, Swift.

'*HATECHI AND DIDI,*' Blowpuff replied.

'**YOU KNOW OUR NAMES?**' said Hatechi in amazement.

Blowpuff's left eyebrow raised.

'*YOU TWO WERE EXTREMELY SUCCESSFUL AT THE ELEMENTAL GAMES. OF COURSE, I KNOW YOUR NAMES.*'

'**OH**,' said Hatechi, strumming his fingers across his chest.

'**OH**,' said Didi, tilting her head forward and allowing her fringe to hide her face. '*ARE WE IN TROUBLE?*'

Blowpuff stifled a snort of laughter.

'*FROM WHAT I HEAR, YOU TWO ARE ALWAYS IN TROUBLE!*'

'**WE CAN GIVE THE MEDALS BACK**,' offered Hatechi.

'**WHATEVER FOR?**' said Blowpuff. '*DID YOU BREAK THE RULES?*'

'*I SUPPOSE IT'S POSSIBLE. THE OLD WRITING IN THE RULE BOOK WAS A BIT DIFFICULT TO UNDERSTAND,*' said Didi.

| ARTISTRY | 16 | STRENGTH | 21 |
| CUTENESS | 57 | CUNNING | 31 |

DRAGON HAWK

| COURAGE | 72 | WISDOM | 66 |
| SPEED | 92 | UNIQUE POWERS | 17 |

Indigenous to Boing Boing, these elusive birds possess the ability to soar at breakneck speeds, second only to Swift the Air Dragon. While they can be challenging to command, those with formidable Artistry prowess may link with them and unleash their full potential. With such unparalleled speed and agility, the **DRAGON HAWK** stands as an ideal candidate for reporting on the goings-on in Alegna.

'*A FRIGHTFUL BORE THAT OLD TEXT. IT SEEMS TO REPEAT ITSELF AN AWFUL LOT,*' said Blowpuff.

'**EXACTLY,**' Didi replied.

'*LET US CONSIDER,*' Blowpuff continued in a contemplative tone. '*IN THE AQUATIC TRIAL, PLUNGE, THE WATER BORE A CONTROLLED CURRENT, WHICH, FORTUITOUSLY, WAS NOT AS VIGOROUS DURING YOUR CONTEST. SUCH CURRENTS ARE PRECISELY WHY OUR ESTEEMED WATER ARTISTRY SCHOLARS TEND TO EXCEL IN THIS EVENT. THEREFORE, NO INFRINGEMENT OF THE*

REGULATIONS OCCURRED THERE. AS FOR THE FLOOR IS LAVA CHALLENGE, THE EDICT PLAINLY STATES THAT NO FOOTWEAR IS ALLOWED. YET, IT MUST BE NOTED THAT MUD DOES NOT QUALIFY AS FOOTWEAR. EVEN IF IT DOES HAVE MAGICAL PROPERTIES.' Blowpuff smiled knowingly. 'MUD SHIELD, NOW THAT WAS IMPRESSIVE. SO IMPRESSIVE, IN FACT, THAT ONLY **MUD ARTISTRY** COULD HAVE BEEN USED, SO AGAIN, NO RULES WERE BROKEN. NOW, THE CHAMBER OF SMOKE WAS A CURIOUS MATTER. THE REGULATIONS, HOWEVER, MAKE NO MENTION OF PROHIBITING THE RIDING OF ANY CREATURE. PRESUMABLY, BECAUSE NO KNOWN ANIMAL THAT COULD FIT INTO THE CHAMBER WOULD HAVE THE STRENGTH TO CARRY CONTESTANTS WHILE NAVIGATING OBSTACLES THROUGH THE THICK SMOKE. APART FROM, OF COURSE, MAYBE A DRAGON. AND WHO IN THEIR RIGHT MIND COULD FATHOM THAT A FORMIDABLE DRAGON WOULD EVER DECIDE TO UNDERTAKE SUCH A FEAT? SURELY NOT THE ARCHITECTS OF THE RULES THEMSELVES.'

Didi and Hatechi's eyes widened. Blowpuff smiled.

'**WHAT IS THE NAME YOU'VE GIVEN HIM?**'

Didi and Hatechi looked around, puzzled.

'*IT CAN BE OUR SECRET,*' Blowpuff continued.

'*KEEP HIM SAFE, AND YOU TWO WILL BE SEEING ME IN THE ALL—ARTISTRY TEMPLE NEXT YEAR.*'

Hatechi and Didi slowly turned to each other and blinked furiously to ensure they were not dreaming. They then grabbed each other and jumped with joy.

'**THE ALL-ARTISTRY TEMPLE!**' they screamed.

'**US! WOO HOO!**'

They stopped abruptly, then turned

LUMBERPRANCER

back to Blowpuff. How could they keep Sherbert
safe when they didn't know where he was?

'WHAT IF WE CAN'T MANAGE TO KEEP HIM SAFE? WOULD WE
NOT BE ALLOWED TO STUDY AT THE ALL-ARTISTRY TEMPLE?'
asked Didi.

'FROM WHAT HE TELLS ME, YOU THREE MAKE QUITE A TEAM,'
Blowpuff smiled.

Hatechi and Didi were more confused than a
Lumberprancer with a sore throat. But before either
could say anything else, a **BURP** came from behind
them.

'**SHERBERT!**' they yelped and turned to see their
slithering friend.

'**SHERBERT**,' Blowpuff chuckled. 'I GUESS IT'S EASIER
TO SAY THAN TERRAGONIS SCUTUMFENDENS LIMOMUCOSUS!'

Hatechi and Didi smothered Sherbert
with cuddles.

'I KNEW YOU'D COME BACK,'
said Hatechi.

'*GUESS WHAT, SHERBERT, NEXT YEAR WE'LL BE STUDYING AT THE ALL—ARTISTRY TEMPLE!*' added Didi.

'**BURP**,' said Sherbert. He then burped three times in succession, causing Hatechi and Didi to exchange a puzzled look.

'*WAIT A DRAGON DARN MINUTE,*' Didi said. '*CAN BLOWPUFF AND SHERBERT UNDERSTAND EACH OTHER?*'

Hatechi and Didi spun around.

'*BLOWPUFF, WHAT DO YOU MEAN SHERBERT TOLD YOU?*' asked Hatechi.

But Blowpuff had vanished.

Didi and Hatechi shrugged, grabbed each other's hands and jumped in circles while chanting,

'**ALL-ARTISTRY TEMPLE! ALL-ARTISTRY TEMPLE!**'

'LITTLE DO THOSE THREE KNOW HOW MUCH TROUBLE IS COMING FOR THEM . . .'

And in that moment, Hatechi and Didi believed their days of adventures were over; no more animal-controlling villains, no more risks from old spells, no more mud cocoons, no more smoke-filled graves, and no more being upstaged by Miss Firey's witty one-liners.

THE TEMPLE OF FUMES

WHO'S THIS?

ZOOMY!

ZOOM TO PAGE 224

Chapter
28

The Last Chapter

(UNTIL THE NEXT BOOK)

Deep in the hills of the Smoke Realm was a temple. This temple was unique. It was constructed from compressed swirling smoke and was known as the **TEMPLE OF FUMES**. It had a large throne room and the throne itself had hypnotic vapour tentacles that moved steadily like overfed snakes. One of the most feared inhabitants of Alegna sat upon this throne, and below him, kneeling on the floor, was Lord Singe.

Lord Singe's head was hung, and his eyes were directed upwards, peeping at the Grand Master of this realm, **EMPEROR SMOKE**, whose long pale white arms protruded from his dark gown. His razor-sharp claw-like fingernails scraped against each other as he spoke.

ZOOMED FROM PAGE 222

THAT IS ALMOST DEFINITELY LORD SINGE.

TRY ZOOMING IN **LOADS.**

ZOOMY

ZOOMY TO PAGE 226

'**AND IN THIS FORM, THE GUMBO DRAGON IS NOT INDESTRUCTIBLE?**' pressed the Emperor.

'*THAT IS CORRECT, YOUR GRACE,*' replied Lord Singe.

Emperor Smoke inhaled slowly and then said a single word that sent shivers down Lord Singe's spine.

'**RJUKA.**'

Lord Singe began to shake as two immense glowing red eyes appeared behind the Emperor. Slowly, through the thickness of the smog, a colossal dragon's head became visible. Sharp spikes jutted from its jaw and black and grey scales glimmered in the dim light as it silently descended.

'*IT WOULD SEEM THAT BLOWPUFF HAS TWO POWERFUL NEW DISCIPLES,*' Emperor Smoke said to the dragon.

'**HOW POWERFUL?**' asked Rjuka the Smoke Dragon, as the deepest, darkest sulphur-laced smoke seeped from its nostrils.

'*THEY DEFEATED LORD SINGE AND THEY HAVEN'T YET BEGUN THEIR TRAINING AT THE ALL-ARTISTRY TEMPLE.*'

ZOOMYED FROM PAGE 224

WOW! WOW! YOU ZOOMYED TOO FAR. BACK, ZOOMY BACK!

'AND HOW EXACTLY DID THESE CHILDREN DEFEAT YOU?' Rjuka demanded.

Lord Singe took small sips of air, trying as hard as he could not to breathe in the toxic sulphur that seeped from Rjuka's nostrils. The red embers of Rjuka's eyes seemed to circle hypnotically in the fog. Lord Singe dared not tell Rjuka that he was defeated by flatulence.

'THEY HOLD SWAY OVER THE GUMBO DRAGON,' Lord Singe managed.

'LEAVE US!' Emperor Smoke demanded, and Lord Singe scrambled to his feet and scurried out.

Emperor Smoke and Rjuka watched him depart.

'I TRUST YOU LISTENED WELL,' said Emperor Smoke.

'EVERY WORD,' replied Rjuka. 'IT SEEMS THAT THE GUMBO DRAGON HAS FOUND A WAY TO DESTROY THE AMULET OF POWER. BY SLOWLY DIGESTING IT, NO LESS!'

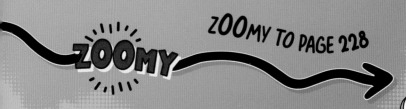

ZOOMY ZOOMY TO PAGE 228

ZOOMY

RJUKA. FIND OUT MORE PAGE 231

EMPEROR SMOKE. FIND OUT MORE PAGE 231

LORD SINGE

'**INDEED**,' said the Emperor. '*ERADICATING SWIFT AND BREAKING THE CIRCLE OF DRAGONS WILL HAVE TO WAIT. A NEW OPPORTUNITY HAS PRESENTED ITSELF.*'

Rjuka shifted in anticipation. Grey fumes swirled around the throne room. Emperor Smoke continued.

'*WE'LL RETRIEVE THE AMULET BY EXPLOITING THE VULNERABILITY IT HAS CREATED IN THE ONCE INDESTRUCTIBLE GUMBO DRAGON.*'

Rjuka hissed in pleasure and opened his wings to leave.

'*CONSIDER IT DONE!*'

'**WAIT!**' Emperor Smoke ordered. '*FIRST, WE DEAL WITH BLOWPUFF'S TWO DISCIPLES!*' Rjuka let out a **ROAR**. Smoke and sulphur fumes filled the room until nothing could be seen apart from the red embers of the mighty dragon's eyes.

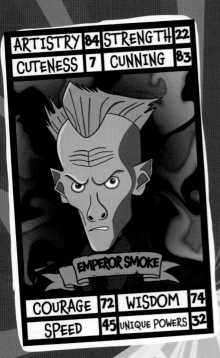

ARTISTRY	84	STRENGTH	22
CUTENESS	7	CUNNING	83

EMPEROR SMOKE

COURAGE	72	WISDOM	74
SPEED	45	UNIQUE POWERS	32

EMPEROR SMOKE.
As the Grand Master of his realm, he commands the very essence of smoke itself, wielding its fickle tendrils to his will. Each Grand Master in their Artistry realm holds sway over their respective dragon, and Emperor Smoke is no exception. However, it is whispered that the malevolent Rjuka, so steeped in wickedness and darkness, is not so easily controlled.

RJUKA breathes a hideously hypnotic sulphur. He hates water, which is a good thing for Alegna because his smoke is the only thing that can harm Quietsch, the Water Dragon

THE CIRCLE OF DRAGONS
RJUKA CAN DEFEAT QUIETSCH.
SWIFT CAN DEFEAT RJUKA.

ARTISTRY	99	STRENGTH	66
CUTENESS	0	CUNNING	87

RJUKA

COURAGE	50	WISDOM	71
SPEED	79	UNIQUE POWERS	42

THE END

AS YOU CAN SEE, I'M NOT ACTUALLY HUMAN; I'M FROM A MAGICAL PLACE CALLED ALEGNA. I OBVIOUSLY DON'T WALK AROUND LOOKING LIKE THIS WHILE I'M ON YOUR PLANET; I USE SOMETHING CALLED A 'FLICKER' TO APPEAR LIKE ONE OF YOU LOVELY LOT. WHEN I FIRST ARRIVED ON EARTH, I WAS SHOCKED BY THE ENVIRONMENTAL POLLUTION THAT PREVENTED ME FROM USING MY ARTISTRY POWERS. THIS DOES MAKE ME WONDER IF ANY OF YOU WOULD HAVE ELEMENTAL POWERS BACK IN ALEGNA.

WHILE TRAVELLING YOUR WORLD, FATE LED ME TO LONDON, WHERE I FOUND TWO EXTRAORDINARY INFANTS THAT HAD BEEN ABDUCTED FROM ALEGNA AND HIDDEN ON EARTH. BEING THE HERO THAT I AM, I RESCUED THEM AND RETURNED THEM TO ALEGNA. THERE, I WATCHED FROM A DISTANCE AS THEY GREW UP IN UNIMAGINABLE WAYS. EVEN I WAS SHOCKED WHEN I FOUND OUT WHO THEY TRULY WERE.

WHAT I WITNESSED OVER THE FOLLOWING YEARS WAS MIND-BLOWING, AND I KNEW THESE STORIES NEEDED DOCUMENTING. HOWEVER, TO DO SO COULD HAVE MEANT GREAT DANGER FOR ALEGNA. SO, I RETURNED TO EARTH TO RECOUNT THEIR EXTRAORDINARY LIVES AS 'FICTION'. I'VE TAKEN UP RESIDENCE NEAR LOCH NESS TO FOCUS ON MY WRITING, AND MY LOYAL DOG, GRUMP, KEEPS ME COMPANY. MY DAYS ARE FILLED WITH VIVID MEMORIES AND THE TASK OF DOCUMENTING THE ADVENTURES OF THESE REMARKABLE CHILDREN, HATECHI AND DIDI.

MY FIRST CHRONICLE GOES BY THE NAME *SHERBERT AND THE PARTLY DIGESTED AMULET OF POWER*. I HOPE YOU ENJOY IT.

 FIND OUT **MORE.**

Battle
Island

The
Desert
Lands

Giants
Quarry

where Onothorn,
n of flames nests.

There are no more
giants

ARTISTRY	4	STRENGTH	35
CUTENESS	66	CUNNING	47

HOODED VULTURE

COURAGE	81	WISDOM	79
SPEED	67	UNIQUE POWERS	32

ARTISTRY	15	STRENGTH	45
CUTENESS	5	CUNNING	77

LORD SINGE

COURAGE	6	WISDOM	26
SPEED	17	UNIQUE POWERS	71

ARTISTRY	78	STRENGTH	23
CUTENESS	24	CUNNING	71

MISS FIREY

COURAGE	84	WISDOM	57
SPEED	39	UNIQUE POWERS	14

ARTISTRY	15	STRENGTH	11
CUTENESS	89	CUNNING	17

SMOKE BAT

COURAGE	31	WISDOM	43
SPEED	78	UNIQUE POWERS	19

ARTISTRY	23	STRENGTH	36
CUTENESS	21	CUNNING	32

GRAHAME

COURAGE	59	WISDOM	13
SPEED	45	UNIQUE POWERS	16

ARTISTRY	46	STRENGTH	10
CUTENESS	87	CUNNING	12

TWO-BUMMED DUCK

COURAGE	81	WISDOM	17
SPEED	17	UNIQUE POWERS	87

ARTISTRY	63	STRENGTH	38
CUTENESS	47	CUNNING	51

MONITOR LIZARD

COURAGE	36	WISDOM	93
SPEED	32	UNIQUE POWERS	71

ARTISTRY	99	STRENGTH	86
CUTENESS	39	CUNNING	12

ONATHORN

COURAGE	87	WISDOM	50
SPEED	69	UNIQUE POWERS	71

ARTISTRY	7	STRENGTH	17
CUTENESS	39	CUNNING	68

ROBBING ROBIN

COURAGE	28	WISDOM	13
SPEED	53	UNIQUE POWERS	59

ARTISTRY	99	STRENGTH	23
CUTENESS	48	CUNNING	26

SWIFT

COURAGE	87	WISDOM	71
SPEED	97	UNIQUE POWERS	76

ARTISTRY	11	STRENGTH	91
CUTENESS	69	CUNNING	10

POLAR BEARATH

COURAGE	79	WISDOM	16
SPEED	21	UNIQUE POWERS	21

ARTISTRY	51	STRENGTH	10
CUTENESS	19	CUNNING	71

CLICKING CROW

COURAGE	14	WISDOM	79
SPEED	53	UNIQUE POWERS	84